The Union 2
Priscilla's Return

A novel by Tremayne Johnson

Also by Tremayne Johnson

A Drug Dealer's Dream

King 1 & 2

The Union

Written by: Tremayne Johnson

Edited by: Tina Nance

Cover design by: Davida (Oddball Dsgn)

Category: Fiction/Urban Life

The Union 2
Priscilla's Return

A novel by Tremayne Johnson

DAVID WEAVER PRESENTS

THE UNION

Priscilla's Return

A NOVEL BY

TREMAYNE JOHNSON

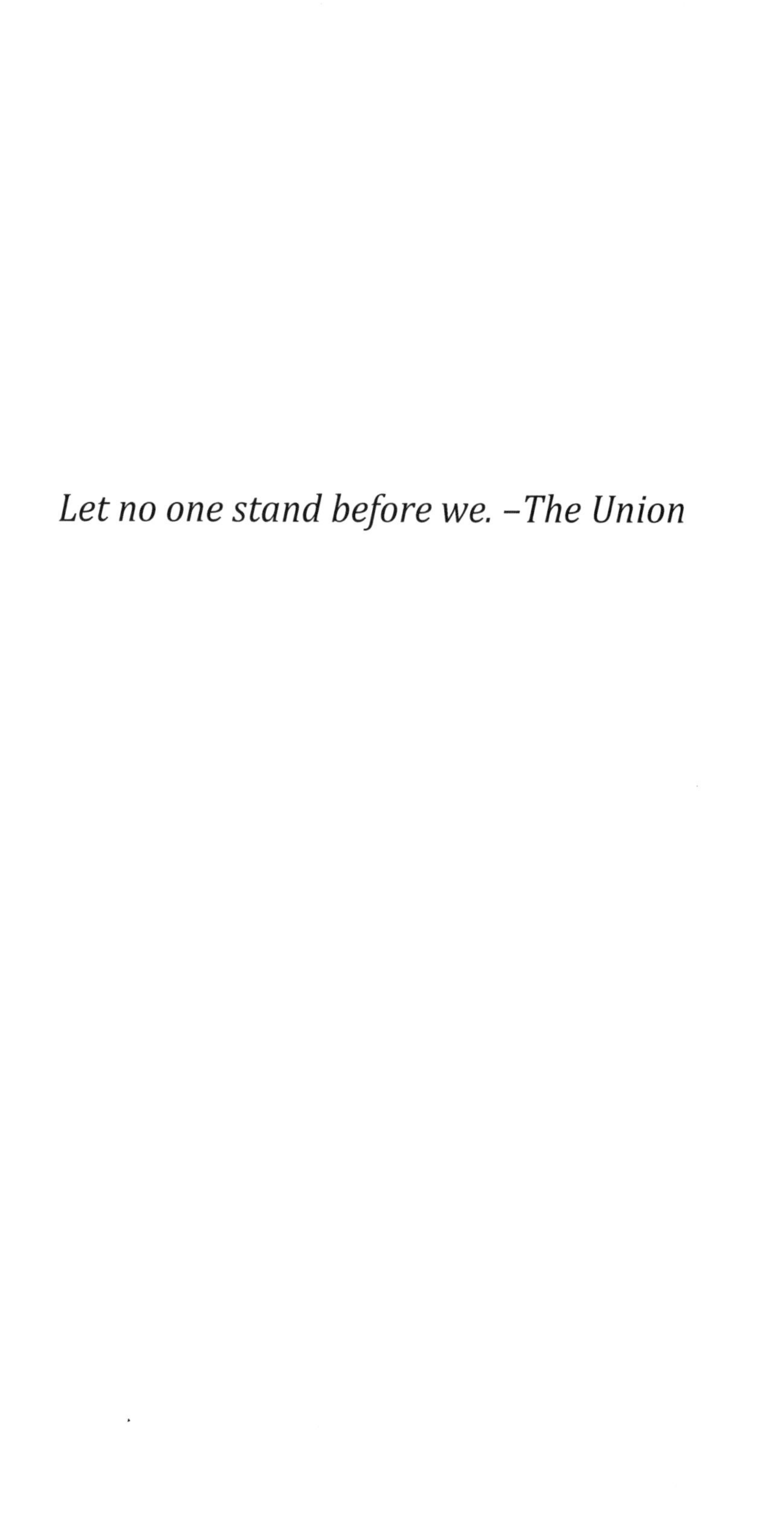

Let no one stand before we. –The Union

This novel is a work of fiction. Any resemblances to real people, living or dead, actual events, establishments, organizations, and/or locales are intended to give the fiction a sense of reality and authenticity. Other names, characters, places and incidents are either products of the author's imagination or are used fictitiously, as are those fictionalized events and incidents that involve real persons and did not occur or are set in the future.

The Union 2
Priscilla's Return

A novel by Tremayne Johnson

CHAPTER ONE

Dr. Callahan rushed into the operating room behind paramedics who had just rolled in Mox's blood soaked body. "Nurse," she called out. "What's his status?"

"Ahh..." The nurse flipped through some papers on a clip board." Twenty-six year old, black male with a gunshot wound to the head."

The heart monitor beeped loudly and the little squiggly lines changed.

"What happened?" the doctor asked.

"I don't know... his BP is decreasing, eighty-nine over sixty." the nurse answered.

Dr. Callahan moved closer to Mox. "Increase the dopamine delivery rate to twelve point five."

"His brain waves are spiking and his blood pressure levels are erratic!" the nurse yelled.

Dr. Callahan stood at the foot of the operating table. He tried to get Mox to speak. "Mox... are you still with us... Mr. Daniels!?"

Mox didn't answer, he couldn't respond.

One of the nurses shouted. "We're losing him... get the crash cart!"

The surrounding chaos agitated Priscilla as she watched the doctors attempt to pump life back into the only man she had ever loved. It was a torturous sight, but she couldn't pull her eyes from it, she hadn't blinked in minutes.

Plastic tubes were inserted into his nose and mouth to help with his breathing and the nurses did whatever was necessary to keep the bleeding to a minimum.

His clothing was cut and ripped from his body and he lay there, naked, on an operating table, fighting for his life.

As the tears hastily cascaded down Priscilla's cheeks she silently prayed to a higher power and begged him not to take Mox. *It wasn't his time,* she thought. This couldn't be a part of what God had planned for her. She had just gotten her life in order and was willing and ready to start over with the hopes of Mox wanting to live as a family. She thought on how long it had been since his easeful touch soothed her tense nerves and made her feel as if there was no one but the two of them on this earth. She dreamed of the day that everything would be right and the three of them could peacefully grow together and get to know each other personally.

Her thoughts drifted and an image of Brandi flashed before Priscilla's eyes. Instantly, an overwrought look of concern flushed her face. *"My baby!"* she shouted, slapping the hard plastic window. *"Mox wake up! Where's Brandi?! Oh my God, where's my baby!?"*

Doctors quickly pulled the shade over the window so no one could see inside, and two tall, dark skinned security guards made their way over to Priscilla. They tried to get her to calm down in an attempt to comfort her, but nothing seemed to work.

Sybil sat in a waiting chair that was pressed against the wall only ten feet away in a distraught trance. Her nerves were ashake and her small palms were clammy. The chatter from the visitors and employees was on mute. Her mind was strained with the events that had so suddenly taken place.

A part of her felt free, but yet she was still extremely saddened at the fact that she had held on to a secret so disheartening and so destructive; a secret she knew would taint, sever or even worse, end her once close relationship with her nephew.

She tried to cry, but the tears just wouldn't fall. Maybe she did have more than a tad bit of animosity towards her sister, more than even *she* believed. Had she been putting on an act, or did she *really* care?

Several thoughts alike raced through her brain faster than Usain Bolt in the 100. She couldn't stop her left leg from shaking. It was a display of fear; an instinct she had been living with her entire life.

Sybil turned her head and saw her brother, Earl, propped against the far wall, one leg up, hands in his pockets and his head down.

"Earl." She whispered.

He looked in her direction; a brief, indistinct look of confusion. "Ain't no fixin' this one, sis." he uttered, shaking his head.

Earl was reluctant to speak openly about the situation, and on top of that, he was getting sick.

Pellets of sweat started to form on his head, his stomach turned and his nerves began twitching. He yawned every few minutes and kept glancing down at his watch and then up at the clock that hung on the wall. He was counting the hours it had been since his last fix. *Seventy-two,* He thought to himself. The diarrhea was about to kick in.

"Shit!" he imagined he was saying it in his head, but it came out loud.

Everyone in the waiting area turned their head to Uncle Wise and he scowled back. "Fuck y'all lookin' at?"

"Earl!" Sybil scolded.

"Fuck that sis, I gotta use the bathroom." He surveyed the large space. "Excuse me; guard… where's the restroom?"

The guard pointed down the long corridor and Earl took off.

Priscilla relaxed her nerves and tried to bring herself together. She looked up at the clock; it read 1:50 pm. Without delay, the panic she had just overcome was slowly settling back in. It almost slipped her mind that she had to report to the shelter by 2-oclock. If she didn't show up or was late, the case worker was going to push her application to the bottom of the pile. She remembered what her counselor in the program, Mrs. James had told before she left.

Priscilla, please don't let me down. These people are expecting you and they're doing me a favor by moving your name to the top of the list. You have to be there by 2:00pm on the day you're released from the treatment center. No if's and's or but's about it. If you don't show up, there's nothing else I can do for you. This is your chance to make the change you've been talking about. Don't screw it up...

Don't screw it up. Don't screw it up! She told herself.

Priscilla turned and looked to the operating room where Mox was. The last thing she wanted to do was leave his side, but it was either that or end up on the streets again. The thought of becoming her old self was frightening enough for her to rationalize and make a quick decision.

She brushed the tears from her face and took a few steps toward Sybil. "Excuse me, Ms. Daniels, I know that right now you're dealing with a lot... I mean... we all are, but I need to find my daughter. Do you know where she is?" she anxiously waited for an answer, but Sybil didn't even raise her head in acknowledgement, she just looked down at the floor. "Ms. Daniels?" Priscilla tried again to get her attention without being rude.

Sybil finally lifted her head; her face, full of grief. "It's all bad, Priscilla... It's all bad."

"I don't understand??" She glanced at the clock again. *What did she mean it was all bad??* Prsicilla's nerves were about to go haywire, but she remained calm. "When was the last time you saw, Brandi?"

Sybil stared into Priscilla's eyes and the affliction was evident. She could tell just by looking at her that she had been through hell and back. The last time she had seen her, Priscilla was strung out on cocaine. She sure didn't look her best. Her hair was ragged, garments were squalid and her spirit was in the mud, but today she was a brand new woman and all she wanted was to see her daughter.

Sybil tried to tell her. "She's gone..."

The words hung in the air for a few seconds before they came down and slapped Priscilla in the face. "Who's gone?" she asked, not believing the words she thought she heard.

"Brandi… is gone, Priscilla… they took her."

Her face went blank. "Took her?" she sat in the chair next to Sybil. "What do mean, they took her… who took her??" her voice was getting louder.

"Excuse me, miss?" One of the guards stepped over to where she sat. "We asked you to keep your voice down… I'm afraid you're going to have to leave."

Priscilla ignored him. "Who took my baby!?" she shouted.

"Miss," The guard went to grab her arm to escort her from the building.

"Get the fuck off me!" she pulled away and faced Sybil. "Who took my baby!?" she cried.

The tears were pouring from her face and her heart felt like it was about to explode through her chest.

Two more guards came around the corner to help ease the situation, but Priscilla was livid. "Miss, you need to calm down before we call the authorities."

Sybil put her head back down and remained silent. She couldn't imagine the anguish and heartache Priscilla was feeling. The only man she had ever loved was stretched out on a bed fighting for his dear life, and her young, innocent daughter was in the custody of child protective services.

"Where's my baby!?" She repeated, trying to grab at Sybil's shirt, but the guard restrained her and had to drag her out of the waiting area and into the street.

Unlike earlier, the shining sun had taken cover behind a fluffy, grey cloud and the gloom had set in. It was still hot, but now the humidity and dankness was making it sticky and uncomfortable. The frustration and displeasure mixed with the heat only heightened Priscilla's anger level. She was confused and didn't have a clue as to where her child was, nobody would tell her anything and to top it off, she had to be at the shelter in 5 minutes.

She bent down to fix her shoe and a cab rolled up to the emergency entrance. After the two passengers got out, Priscilla begged the driver to drop her off a few blocks over. When she got settled in she would have to contact her mother to find out if she knew anything about where Brandi was.

The two and a half block ride took only a few minutes, but when Priscilla burst through the Providence house doors at 89 Sickles Avenue, the clock read; 2:05.

She cursed under her breath, *shit!* She was late.

An older, brown skinned, heavy set woman with black shoulder length hair sat behind a desk rambling into a cordless phone about her baby's father not paying child support. She paused in the middle of her conversation. "You're late."

Priscilla froze, her mouth opened, but nothing came out.

"Yeah, girl... I'll call you back." she rolled her eyes at Priscilla. "Umm hmm... my two-o-clock finally decided to stroll in." she clicked.

"I'm sorry. My name is Priscilla Da—"

"Ms. Davis," She cut in. "Like I said, you're late. You see that clock?" She turned and pointed at the clock on the wall behind her. "It says two-oh-five and your appointment was scheduled for two-o-clock. That means you should have been here fifteen minutes ago. I'm sure they told you about being *on time* in the program."

Priscilla started to say something, but got cut off again.

"You know... you're lucky Mrs. James and I are cool." She reached into a cabinet and grabbed a small stack of papers. "Usually, you would have come through that door late and I would have kindly told you to turn it right around. Are you serious about this?" she asked.

"Yes, very serious... and again, I'm sorry for being late."

The woman sucked her teeth and shook her head. She had seen a thousand Priscillas walk through that door. "Sorry ain't gone get you nowhere in this world, so that's the first thing you need to do..." she placed the papers in a clipboard and pushed it toward Priscilla. "Stop being sorry and be responsible. Chile' don't nobody owe you a damn thing, so don't expect anything, and you won't be disappointed. Now, I don't know your situation or the things you been through in life, but let me tell you this..." she looked directly at Priscilla. "You can't help *nobody* if you don't help *yourself* first... and that's the truth. It took me a long time to figure that one out."

Priscilla listened closely to every word that was said. She watched the woman's body language and it was like this woman knew exactly how she was feeling, like she understood what she had been through, like she had walked in these same shoes some time ago.

She stepped closer to the desk, grabbed the pen and started to fill out the questionnaire. Her emotions were chaotic and the pressures of life felt like a ton of cement bricks on her shoulders. No longer able to hold it up, she broke down and a tear drop slowly descended her cheek. It splashed the paper she was writing on.

"God, please help me..." she whispered.

The woman came from behind the desk and grabbed Priscilla's hands to console her. Her palms were warm, moist and shaky from anxiety. "Listen baby, we're gonna help you. I don't want you to think I was trying to come down on you or belittle you in any type of way. I just have to give it to you the same way somebody else who stood behind that desk gave it to me..."

Priscilla lifted her head. "You—?"

"Yup, *me*... I was just like *you*. It was ten years ago when I came strolling on through that door." She nodded toward the entrance. "Young, disrespectful with a heart full of hate and a heavy addiction to heroin. I was bad... and now, I'm sitting here looking at you and I know you're a good person. I can see it. You got a good heart; all you need is some guidance. If you're willing to put forth the effort, we will assist you in reaching your goals." She let go of Priscilla's hands and walked back behind the desk. "It's all up to you."

CHAPTER TWO

The black Town Car barreled down the block and then skidded to a stop on Webster Avenue and Krest. Cleo knew who the driver of the vehicle was, but after what just happened, he was nervous and extremely cautious.

"What the fuck took you so long, Chris?" He jumped into the backseat and pulled the door closed.

"There was traffic Cleo." Chris put the car in reverse and quickly made an illegal U turn. "I got here as fast as I could."

Cleo stretched across the backseat and tried to regain control of his breathing. The humidity had him drenched in sweat and red splatters of blood looked like ink blots on his grey t-shirt.

"You alright back there?" Chris asked. He kept glancing in the rearview mirror.

Cleo grimaced. "Yeah, why?"

"I mean... you are back there breathing hard and sweating profusely... and you do have some blood on your shirt."

"Oh, you mister funny man, today, huh?"

"Naw... not like that Cleo. I'm jus' sayin'."

"What the fuck you sayin'?" He sat up in the seat, but Chris kept silent. "That's what the fuck I thought. No, I'm not alright." Cleo wasn't playing at all today.

"Is there anything I can do for you?"

"Yeah Chris... shut the fuck up and drive the car. Take me to Vito's."

Twenty minutes later, the sleek Town Car pulled up to the sidewalk in front of the Bar & Grill, but before Cleo exited, he checked his weapon. He gripped the handle firmly and then looked down at the blood on his hands.

It was Mox's blood.

A voice in his head whispered, *why?* But he pushed it from his thoughts and stepped out into the warm, moist, summer air.

Cleo was agitated and confused at first, but when he thought about the situation rationally, he came to the conclusion that there was only be one person that could have leaked that missing surveillance tape. For a short minute, he even considered storming into Vito's and blatantly opening fire on whoever was within distance, but what good would that do? So, on the ride over, he presumed that Vinny Telesco was the only one that could get him away from all the trouble that was shadowing him, and he needed to see him face to face.

As he stepped closer to the entrance, Cleo's mind was so clouded that he wasn't aware of his surroundings and missed the county police car that was parked two spaces up.

He pushed the door open to Vito's and walked in.

The music played at a very low volume and the atmosphere was sedate. Three patrons sat casually on stools along the front of the bar, watching an old war movie on the flat screen while Tony, the bartender, fixed up another round. He turned when he heard the bells on the door jingle.

"Aye, Tony wassup?" Cleo waved, but didn't break his stride. He continued straight to the back.

Tony tried to stop him. "Hey, you can't go back there!" But his words fell on deaf ears.

Cleo walked past the tables nodding his head at the few customers who sat eating and advanced to the back of the restaurant. He came to a stop when he spotted a small crowd of people sitting at a large table and three dark suited henchmen standing off to the left; two dark haired and one dirty blonde. But his focus solely lied upon Vinny Telesco's pale, wrinkled face.

Their eyes locked and Vinny made a gesture to his goons who quickly stepped over to where Cleo stood. "Pat 'em down." he said, rising from his seat.

One of the dark haired henchmen felt Cleo's waist and removed the pistol he had tucked. "Why'd you leak the tape, Vinny!?" Cleo shouted.

"Fuck you and that tape, Cleo." The few guests who sat at the table started to get up and leave. "Everybody sit down. This won't take long."

After Cleo killed Casey in the hotel, he knew the only way the police could identify him was by the surveillance tape, so he reached out to the mob boss because of his strong ties to the city and magically the tape came up missing. Cleo then swore to an agreement with Vinny that the tape would be destroyed in exchange for a million dollars, but Cleo couldn't come up with the money. A second chance was given when Vinny ordered him to kill Mox, but again, Cleo didn't produce and The Old Man felt like his hand had been forced.

"All the work I put in for you, and this how you treat me? We had an agreement about that tape. You broke your promise, Vinny."

"No, you didn't produce; besides... promises are made to be broken." He raised his eyebrows at his men and they snatched Cleo up from both sides.

There was no fighting it, he was outnumbered. The mob boss got within an inch of his face. "You know, Cleo... you got some fuckin' nerve comin' here." his voice was dry, and hoarse. "First of all, you're interruptin' my fuckin' wine and cheese party." Two of the guest smirked, but this was far from a laughing matter. "I trusted you with my family and what did I get!?" his voice went as loud as he could get it. "Huh, what did *I* get, Cleo? You know what *I* got... a dead fuckin' son, that's what!" Vinny looked to his left. "Mikey, teach this fuckin' guy a lesson."

Cleo looked to the right and Mikey scowled at him. "What's up, Cleo?" He sounded clogged and stuffed up because he had gauze wrapped around his face to protect his nose from when Mox hit him with the gun.

Sensing the situation was about to take a turn for the worse, Cleo tried to reason. "Vinny, wait... I did it... I killed, Mox."

The Old Man smiled, fixed his suit jacket and then returned to his seat. "So you come here for what; a trophy or somethin'?" a dry giggle escaped his mouth, but the flame in his eyes told another story. "It's too late, Cleo." He sat back, crossed his right leg over his left and waited.

The sound that the ten inch Falcon Stiletto folding knife made when Mikey flipped it open caused Cleo to twist his neck in an attempt to see what it was. The glare from the track lighting that hung fifteen feet in the air hit the stainless steel blade and made it glimmer.

Cleo's eyes grew wide.

Mikey gripped the mirror finish wood handle tightly with revenge the only thought on his mind. It was weighing on him so heavy, that recently he become depressed and eagerly violent, which was unlike him. He painfully wanted to avenge his brother's death and the only thing preventing a homicide this evening would be the county police officer who was standing by the entrance waiting on an order of pasta.

"You scarred my family for life when you killed my little brother." He said, taking a few steps closer to Cleo. "And since I can't kill you right now... I'ma leave you wit' a scar to remember me by until I catch up to you again."

Cleo kept his focus on the knife. "I ain't have nothin' to do wit' your brother's murder."

Mikey ignored his words and placed the razor-sharped blade to the side of Cleo's face. "Every time you take a look in a mirror, you'll be reminded of why you shouldn't fuck wit' the Telesco's."

He slowly dragged the blade south, from his forehead to the bottom of his chin and as soon as he lifted his hand, Cleo's face opened up like a baked potato split down the middle with butter and sour cream topping.

The high pitched howl he let out was ear wrenching.

He tried to break away, but as big as he was, Cleo still couldn't fight his way out the grasps of Vinny's henchmen.

A stream of blood raced down his chest from the wound and his tongue could literally be seen through the side of his cheek.

The police officer heard the shriek, looked up, and started to walk to the back, but Vinny waved his hand assuring him that everything was okay. He had an idea of what was going on, but he and the Telesco's were like family. Even though he was very aware of their business, he did his best to turn a blind eye to it.

"You've been nothin' but problems lately, Cleo." Vinny got up. "Gimme that." he grabbed the knife from Mikey. "I know you heard that old saying, 'never bite the hand that feeds you'... well, you bit me once and I sure won't give you the chance to do it again."

The dirty blonde haired henchman gripped Cleo's wrist and slammed his hand down on the table.

Vinny clutched the knife firmly between his fingers, lifted it and smashed the sharp-edged blade into the back of Cleo's right hand.

The pain shot through his arm and instantly he felt the discomfort through his whole body, but he didn't make a sound. He just gazed into Vinny's passionless eyes searching for a speck of endearment, but nothing was there.

The only thing positive about this situation was that Cleo knew Vinny wouldn't have him killed right now. It was too many witnesses.

The Old Man yanked the knife out of his hand, wiped the blood onto Cleo's shirt and said, "Get this piece-a-shit outta my face."

Two of the henchmen pulled Cleo by his arms and pushed him out the front door.

Stumbling to his feet, he barely made it back to the Town Car before he mumbled. "Drive, Chris." He pulled the door shut with his good hand and his wounded hand was wrapped up in his t-shirt, but the bleeding was getting heavier.

Chris wasted no time. He started the car, threw it in drive and peeled from the scene. When he checked the rearview mirror he saw all the blood on Cleo's shirt. It was definitely more than what had been there before. "Oh shit! What the hell??... we gotta get you to a hospital... Cleo, you alright?"

"No hospitals, Chris... jus' drive." He looked down at the dime sized hole in his hand and could almost see right through it.

"Here, take these." Chris tossed the two hand towels he kept in the glove compartment into the backseat with Cleo. "Use them to slow up the blood flow. Just wrap it around your hand and squeeze it."

Cleo wanted to smile, but just the thought of it made his face hurt. "You a fuckin' doctor now, Chris?"

"Naw, but I saw someone do it on that television show, *Survivor*. It works, trust me."

"Trust will get you killed, Chris."

The Town Car veered to the right and went down the ramp and onto the highway.

"Okay, listen. I know somebody who could help you out right now. You know, fix you up. No hospitals. No police; none of that."

"Get me there... and Chris," Cleo paused and looked in disgust at his reflection in the partition as small droplets of blood continued to fall from his chin. "If it aint what you say it is... I'ma kill you."

CHAPTER THREE

"Yes, daddy! Oooh! Have it baby... this pussy yours, Franky!" Toya bellowed; arching her back and rotating her 46 inch, lemon colored hips while Frank plugged her from behind. "Beat this pussy up, daddy... ohhhhh!"

The distinctly, alluring 26 year old Latoya Reid is a 6 foot, 165 pound redbone with straight, long black hair that hangs to the middle of her back. She has grey, cat-like eyes, a bunch of freckles spread out across the top of her rosy cheeks and an ass that belongs in *Straight Stuntin'* Magazine.

Her sunny colored complexion makes her look like she's of foreign descent, but the reality is, she's just an old country girl from the deep southern woods of South Carolina who migrated to New York in pursuit of a dream.

She and Frank met on the set of a video that she had been hired to perform in, and ever since that day, he's been knocking it down.

"Who pussy is this? Who pussy is this?..." Frank thrust his pelvis back and forth, sliding his 9 ½ inches as far into Toya's vagina as possible. "This *my* pussy!"

"Yes!" She screamed. "Go deep daddy... ohhhhh, yeah... take this pussy! Take this puussssyyy!" Toya's walls were contracting and the sensational pleasures she was feeling were quite uncommon for her. She came back to back to back, releasing her creamy white frosting all over Frank's dick.

A sheer coat of sweat covered his body as he physically punished Toya's love box.

His hands were placed at the small of her back in a diamond like position so he could control all movement.

He looked down at her soft, pretty ass sliding on his glistening dick and smiled.

Beads of perspiration slipped from his forehead and onto her ass cheeks as he worked the middle.

All those late nights in the gym is paying off.

His stamina was at its highest level and his performance was at its peak.

He stood up on his tippy toes and submerged himself in the pussy.

"Ohhhhhh!" Toya moaned. "That shit is deeeeppp, daddy! Ummmm..."

Frank grabbed her by the waistline and in a sequential cadence he rammed his power rod between her vaginal lips. "Say my name, girl! Tell me who run this muthafucka!"

Toya could barely catch her breath to speak. "Fraaa—"

"Say my name, girl!"

"Fraaann—" She still couldn't get it out.

Her shrieks of pure joy grew louder and all you could hear was skin slapping, heavy panting and the headboard of Frank's $3000 queen sized bed banging against the wall.

"Say it, girl!"

"Frrraaannnkyyy, baaaabbbyyyy!!"

Frank backed up, rolled the condom off his dick and splashed a load of cum all over Toya's ass. "Ahhhhhh!" he spanked her cheeks until he released the last drop and then he fell onto the bed beside her.

His cellphone rang, but he noticed that it was on the opposite side of the bed and out of reach. "Answer that for me." he said.

Toya looked at him, rolled her eyes and picked the phone up off the nightstand. "Hello?"

The caller replied. "Lemme speak to Frank."

"Who dis?"

"Bitch, put Frank on the phone!"

Toya sucked her teeth. “Here, nigga.” She dropped the phone on Frank’s chest and he pressed the speaker button.

“Hello?”

“You lettin’ bitches answer your phone now?”

Toya’s lip turned up. “Bitches?”

“Yeah, you heard me, video hoe.”

“Fuck you, nigga!”

Frank grabbed the phone, took it off speaker and looked at Toya. “Yo, chill.”

“Fuck that... you jus’ gon’ sit there and let that nigga call me all types a’ bitches... fuck you too!” She got up and walked out the room.

Frank sat up in the bed. “Nate what up?”

“I need to see you.”

“Why, wassup?”

“Shit got crazy... somebody hit Mox.”

“What!?”

“Word... said he got hit in the head. It’s ugly right now.”

Frank’s lip dropped and the phone fell from his grasp, hitting the carpet.

The only people he could think of that were capable of something like this were the Italians.

His head slumped and he stared down at the phone. He could hear Nate calling for him, but his mind was someplace else.

Mox was like a brother to Frank and the rest of the team, and if it meant going to war with the Italians, then bodies were about to drop because regardless of stature, creed or street ranking; nobody touched a Union affiliate and got away with it.

Frustration, anger and pure ignorance clouded his thoughts as he reached for the phone. "Somebody gotta bleed, Nate. They touch one of ours, we touch one of theirs. You know how this shit go."

Nate felt the exact same way, but the question was, who was getting touched?

"Yeah, I feel you, but who?"

"Those fuckin' Italians, who else..." Frank answered.

"Nah, Frank… this shit happened in the hood. I know the Italians got balls, but them shits ain't that big and them muthafuckas ain't just gunnin' niggas down in the hood like that."

Frank took a minute to think about what Nate was saying. "Okay…" he nodded his head in agreement. "You might be right about that." he tried to think about any other instances where they may have had an altercation with someone a while back, but nothing came to mind. "You spoke to Cleo?"

"Not at all, but what you wanna do about *this?* I'm on my way to New Ro right now."

Frank wiped his face in confusion, because for a second he thought he was dreaming. But when Toya stepped back into the room, he knew shit was real.

She was still upset about Nate calling her out her name. "I can't believe you sat there and let that nigga call me a bitch."

If she was paying attention, she would have clearly seen the discomforting look of annoyance plastered on Frank's grill. "Leave it alone, Toya." he warned.

"Leave it alone?" Her eyebrows rose. "What the fuck you mean, *leave it alone?* This nigg—"

Frank leaped from the bed and cut her off in mid-sentence. "I said let it go, Toya!" his face was flush with tears.

She was shocked.

Her mouth hung open and her eyes were stuck to Frank's face. "I... I..." she didn't know what to say, but Frank let it be known.

"Mox got shot." The words didn't even feel right coming off his tongue.

"What?... Oh, no... I'm sorry, baby." Toya heard the convulsion in Frank's voice and felt sympathy and deep sorrow for him, Mox and the whole Daniels family.

She liked Mox and had actually been given the chance to meet him one night in Frank's club a couple weeks back. At first impression, she was awed at how someone of his eminence could present himself in such a reposeful and unruffled fashion.

According to the stories she had been hearing, this guy Mox was being portrayed as some type of brash, gun toting, drug dealer, killing machine, but from her observation she saw he was just a young, street nigga with a good head on his shoulders. Combined with the discipline to abide by a set of principles and the determination to get what he wanted, Mox's leadership qualities were easily recognized by strangers.

Frank picked his pants up and started to put them on. "I gotta go." he said.

"Wait..." Toya grabbed his hand. He was shaking. "Baby, where you going?"

Frank pulled away, ignored her question and went to the closet to get his gun.

"Frank, please don't leave." She begged, watching him check the clip.

He placed the gun in his waistband and threw on a three-button, short sleeve Polo shirt. "That's my brother, Toya. What you expect me to do?" he snatched his car keys off the table and stormed out of the house.

There was nothing more she could say or do; Frank had his mind made up.

Toya watched from the second floor window as he got into his car and drove away. She cried and silently prayed that everything would be okay, but deep within her gut she knew that was a far distance from the truth.

Tupac's expressive, true-to-life lyrics trumpeted through the Bose stereo system as Frank clutched the wheel with one hand and held a lit blunt in the other. He let the thick ghost like smoke flow through his nostrils while he kept his eyes glued to the road.

Pac's vocals were mesmeric.

My Ambitionz Az A Ridah...

The sleek black 500 Benz hugged the road as Frank pushed the machine to speeds reaching close to one hundred miles an hour. By the time the blunt was done, he was cruising down Horton Avenue, pulling up to the projects.

It was 7:15 pm and the sun was just beginning to set. The dull, red and yellowish rays produced an orange glow that hovered over the projects and the lingering smell of death was afloat throughout the air.

Whether it was a shooting, stabbing, fist fight or just a heated argument, whenever there was an incident in the hood, everybody came outside to be nosy and this night was no different.

The past three days had produced two shootings; one, a murder and the other had yet to be told. Who would have thought that the summer was just beginning to blossom?

Frank stepped from the vehicle and made his way down the strip towards the buildings. When he passed the park area, he was approached by a young kid on a pedal bike.

"Yo, whats good?" The kid said.

Frank slowed his stride to get a good look at the kid. "You know me?" he replied.

He knew something was up with him because it was eighty degrees outside and this kid had on shorts and a black hoodie.

The kid on the bike sped up and cut Frank off before he could get any further down the strip. He jumped off the Mongoose and Frank went to reach for his weapon.

"Yo, chill homie… it aint like that." The kid extended his hand. "Tyrell Michaels. I'm Dana's lil' cousin." he pulled his hand back when he saw Frank wasn't budging. "You Mox peoples, right?"

"Yeah, why?"

"Your man Nate jus' went upstairs. C'mon, I'll show you where it's at."

Frank had met Dana before, but had never been to her house. The kid didn't sound like he was trying to pull a stunt so he followed him into the building.

When they got to the door, Tyrell knocked twice and someone shouted from the inside. "Who is it?"

"It's me, cousin."

When door came open, they walked into the apartment and Frank immediately noticed that Dana had been crying. Her make-up was smeared all over her face from wiping away tears.

The strong stench of cigarette smoke lingered in the atmosphere and clouded the room.

Frank saw Nate sitting on the sofa smoking a Newport and shook his head. "I thought you quit?" He asked?

Nate took a long drag and exhaled the smoke. "I did, but this fuckin' stress is killin' me Frank."

"Jus' be cool. We gon' handle this accordingly. First I need to know what happened... Did anybody speak to Cleo?"

Dana and Tyrell looked at each other and at the same time said, *"Cleo?"*

"You don't watch the news do you?" Tyrell grabbed the remote and hit the power button.

The breaking news story had been playing all day and as soon as they showed Casey's face on the screen, Dana broke down and ran to the back room.

Nate stood up off the sofa and he and Frank stared at the television. The staggering looks on their faces told stories of their own and neither of them wanted to believe that what they were seeing was real, but the harsh realities of life aren't always the most pleasant, especially when you're dealing with these cold and bitter streets.

"Are you fuckin' serious!?" Frank was livid.

Nate pulled another cigarette from his pack and lit it. "I knew that mutha-fucka was a snake." he puffed the stogie and let the toxins enter his lungs.

"Yo, listen." Tyrell turned the television off and took a seat on the folding chair. "It's on fire out here right now, fam. My lil' man jus' got booked for a body yesterday and this shit wit' Mox this morning jus' added more fuel to the flame. Niggas said Cleo hit Mox too."

For a few seconds silence filled the room.

"This shit went all the way to the left, Frank." Nate was pacing now.

"What hospital they got my boy in?" Frank questioned.

His stomach was in knots and tears were building in the well of his eyes, but he knew this wasn't the place or time to show emotion.

"He up the block at *Sound Shore* right now." Tyrell answered. "Yo," He sat on the sofa and whispered. "I know the spot Cleo be at. That nigga go there at least once a week to trick off... I can handle that for you."

"Handle what?" Nate didn't like outsiders intervening in family business.

Tyrell felt the vibe and tried to ease the tension. "Mox was like family to me too... even though we had our differences, I know everything he was telling me was to help me. He wanted me to stay in the books and stay off the block, but I a'int listen. Anyway... this is the shit I'm here for." he reached under the sofa and pulled out his taped up .38 revolver. "Mox looked out and bailed me, my cousin and my homeboy out of jail a few days ago. I got love for that dude, so if some work gotta be put in..." he paused and looked at their faces. "All I'm saying is; I'm that nigga to get the job done."

Frank realized Tyrell was the one who got Dana's house raided and Brandi taken away, he probably felt like he owed Mox.

Nate wasn't feeling it. "All you young niggas want is a name for yourself. We don't need no other niggas handlin' our busi—"

Frank jumped in. "hol' up Nate..." he eyed Tyrell. "lil' nigga say he ready to put in work, let's see what he about."

Nate looked Tyrell up and down. He of all people knew that shooters came in all shapes and sizes and the only way to find out if his word was authentic was to give him a chance. He wasn't one hundred percent sure if giving Tyrell the green light was the right decision, but in his book everybody deserved a shot.

"Fuck it... you only get one chance to make a first impression, kid. I hope you make it a good one."

They went to leave out and Frank stopped at the door. He glanced down at the old, rusted .38 Tyrell had in his hand.

"You gon' need something better than that to put in work." He grabbed the silver Baretta .380 semi-automatic off his waistline and tossed it on the couch.

Tyrell placed the old .38 on the coffee table and picked up the .380. He gripped the wood grain handle tightly. "This is that Canadian joint, right here?"

Frank and Nate wore surprised looks.

"You know your weapons, huh?" Nate reached around his waist, lifted his shirt and grabbed the pistol from the small of his back. He tossed it on the couch next to Tyrell.

He palmed the lightweight, chrome and black handgun. "Ooh, this is that new G2 right here... and it's a forty." Tyrell studied the gun. "It got the good thumb rest, a new trigger safety," he held the weapon with two hands, extended his arm and aimed at an invisible target. "This is that shit the police be using." he pressed a button on the handle and the clip fell from the bottom. "I know my ratchets" he cocked the barrel, put his nose to it and sniffed. "Brand new." he said, placing it on the table.

Nate smiled for the first time. "Impressive, kid. Keep it."

The door slammed and Frank and Nate were gone, leaving Tyrell on his cousin's couch with three guns and the green light to put a hole in Cleo's head.

He sat back, spread his arms across the back of the sofa and the corners of his mouth almost touched his ears.

Less than 72 hours ago, Tyrell was broke, homeless and unaware of where his next meal was coming from, but now he was sitting on a couple thousand stacks, two brand new guns and a chance to earn the trust of Mox's comrades.

Who says crime don't pay?

CHAPTER FOUR

Wise Earl jumped from the seat he was sitting in and approached Doctor Callahan as he exited the operating room. "Doctor, please tell us you got some good news?"

The doctor removed the mask from his face, peeled his gloves off, and took a seat between Earl and Sybil. "I would be lying to you if I told you everything was going to be okay. Your nephew has suffered a severe gunshot wound to head." he stood up, pulled an x-ray from his clipboard and held it up to the light so Sybil and Earl could see it. "This right here is an x-ray of your nephew's skull. As you can see," he pointed to what looked to be a small hole. "Right here is where the bullet entered."

Earl stepped in closer to get a better view of the x-ray. "So, where did it come out?" he questioned.

"That's the problem." Doctor Callahan removed his glasses and tried to explain what happened. "See, the bullet traveled along the midline of his brain and now it's lodged back here," he pointed. "in the base of his skull."

"So, what that mean?" Earl was getting agitated. "You still a'int tellin' us nothin'"

Doctor Callahan placed his glasses back on his face. "Mr. Daniels, if we go in and try to remove that bullet from Mox's skull there's more than a fifty percent chance that he could die under the knife."

"Oh my God!"

The tears came falling from Sybil's eyes as she slumped to the floor. The last thing she wanted to believe was that she was the cause of all this turmoil, but the truth is an uncomfortable actuality and in time, all untruth hiding in darkness will be illuminated and unmasked.

Earl picked Sybil up, wrapped his arms around her, and did what he could to tranquilize her discomfort. He was sensitive and sympathetic to her misery because he knew exactly how it felt to be the cause of something tragic; there were demons in his closet too.

"Is there *any* good news, Doc?" Earl asked.

"The good news is, Mox's heart is still beating. The bad news... his brain is severely damaged."

"A *coma?*"

"Yes," Doctor Callahan lifted the x-ray again to show Earl. "When the bullet entered the skull, it damaged these areas right here." He pointed. "Damage to these parts of the brain can sometimes result in amnesia or dementia."

"So, you tellin' me that when he wake up he a'int gon' remember what happened?"

"If and when he wakes up... memory loss is a possibility. I'm sorry Mr. and Ms. Daniels, but that's all the information I can give you at the moment. We'll continue to do everything we can to keep Mox alive. You got my word on that." he turned to leave.

"Doc, hol' up." Earl caught up to him before he got too far down the hall. "How long you think he gon' be in this coma?"

Doctor Callahan shook his head. "I don't know, Mr. Daniels... could be one day, could be one year. It's all up to Mox. If he fights, I'm sure he can make it."

Earl watched as the doctor turned on his heels and continued down the corridor. He made his way back to where Sybil sat in the waiting area.

"Excuse me nurse," he called to a young lady who had just left out of the room they moved Mox into. "Is it possible we can see my nephew now?"

The young nurse looked down at her watch. "Sure, you've got twenty minutes until visiting hours are up, but before you go in there, let me tell you; he's not responsive and it looks a lot worse than it really is."

Earl ignored her warning and went to get Sybil to come with him into Mox's room. "Sis, c'mon, they said we got twenty minutes."

She sat still for a second and then got up and they walked toward the room holding hands, but before they could get inside, Sybil panicked. "I can't do this!" she snatched her hand from Earl, ran back to where she was sitting, buried her face in her lap, and cried.

Earl was fifteen feet away from the room, but it felt like he was taking a thousand steps to get there. His heartbeat sped up and he kept swallowing saliva. The closer he got to the door, the more real it seemed.

He turned the knob and slowly pushed the door open.

The medium sized room was painted sky blue and there were two beds, but one was empty.

A quick glance around the room and Earl's his eyes fell on the heart monitor next to the occupied bed.

Beep... Beep... Beep...

The frigid temperature in the room and the eerie sounds coming from the machines gave Earl the chills.

Next to the heart monitor was an oxygen machine, an IV and a breathing module.

"Damn, baby boy..." Earl could barely look at Mox.

He was lying on his back, his head was wrapped in gauze and his arms were straight at his side.

Earl took a few steps closer and the repulsive sight of Mox's swelled face numbed his nerves and churned his insides.

He gagged and a warm sensation rose in his chest causing him to grab at his stomach and reach for the trash can. He wanted to vomit, but nothing came up.

Earl wiped the saliva that hung from his lip and tried to bear the emotional scene.

The beeping of the heart monitor sounded like it was getting louder by the seconds.

Beep... Beep... Beep...

"Damn, nephew..." Earl finally managed to get to the chair that was beside Mox's bed.

He sat down and stared at the tubes that were in his nose and mouth and a tear casually slid down the side of his face. "C'mon, baby boy, you gotta wake up." he whispered. "We need you out here Mox. Your family needs you. You gotta fight nephew." the tears started to fall with ease. "Mox, I'm sorry..." Earl cried his heart out and begged God to help Mox recover.

He felt someone else's presence in the room and thought it was his sister. When he turned to look, it was Frank and Nate standing in the doorway.

Frank was waiting for Mox to jump up from the bed smiling and tell everyone that this whole thing was a joke, but that didn't happen.

He tried to move, but his legs were frozen.

"You gotta take care of this Frank." Earl sobbed.

Frank's eyes were already watery from seeing Mox lying in that hospital bed, but when he saw Earl crying like a child, it only intensified his aggravation.

He brushed the dampness from his eyes and looked at Earl. "Let no one stand before we." He mumbled and then he and Nate exited the hospital.

Priscilla's first overnight stay in the shelter felt like one of the longest days of her life. For weeks she sat in the inpatient program dreaming of the day she would be able to hold her daughter again, only to come home and hear that she's gone.

Sitting on her cot with her arms wrapped around her knees, pressed against her chest, she closed her eyes and thought back on the day's events.

A whirlwind of emotions spun inside of her and the attempt to suppress the pain was useless. She could no longer hide how she was feeling.

The tears came down like a waterfall.

Priscilla opened her eyes and looked around the large room.

The nasty colored green walls made her insides quiver and the fetid stench of old, dirty clothes clogged the air.

Damn, I gotta pee

She stepped off the cot and walked down the dark isle of the dorm to the restroom and in passing, she counted the cots aligned alongside the walls. It was twelve on each side, but two were empty.

When she pushed the door open a thick cloud of smoke smacked her in the face and made her lip turn.

She heard movement, and one of the stall doors flew open. A tall, slim, brown skinned female with bulging eyes and ashy lips came stumbling out.

"Oh," She sucked her teeth. "it's jus' the new girl. We cool… right?" she inquired.

Priscilla stared at the scraggily woman. She was high, disheveled and very edgy. "I don't care what y'all do in here. I jus' came to use the bathroom."

Another woman stepped out the stall. "She bedda mind her muthafuckin' business." She stopped in front of Priscilla. "Bitch, you fuckin' up my nut."

Priscilla acted like she didn't know what was going on. "Huh? I jus' came to pee." She tried to get around the woman and go into the stall, but she was much bigger than Priscilla. "Excuse me."

"You a pretty bitch a'int you." She went to touch the side of her face, but Priscilla moved. "You sure you don't want me to come in there wit' you?"

Priscilla wasn't surprised at the advance, her thought was that it may have come a little later than sooner, but she was anticipating it. Her girl Jennifer, had already schooled her to most of the occurrences that would take place in these shelters.

She tried to mentally prepare Priscilla for what she was about to encounter, because living in these shelters was very similar to living in prison. The major difference was; staying at the shelter was a personal choice. You didn't have to be there if you didn't want to.

She ignored the heavy set woman's words and nudged her way past the two females and into the stall.

The crummy bathroom was typical of a government facility. It reeked of sour urine and feces and the toilet seat was stained with dry blood.

Nasty bitches.

When she exited the stall, the slim, brown skinned chick was leaning against the sink puffing on a cigarette.

"What's yo' name?" She blew smoke out and tapped the ash in the sink.

"Priscilla." She replied.

"Umm hmm... well, my name is Kim and that bitch there," she said pointing to the door. "That was Mother Nature... she run this shit. If I was you, I wouldn't get on her bad side; she known to have a not so very good temper." Kim offered the remains of her cigarette to Priscilla.

"No thank you. I don't smoke."

She finished washing her hands and went to grab a paper towel from the dispenser, but Kim blocked her. "Bitch, you actin' like you too good to smoke wit' me?"

Priscilla snapped, snatched a handful of Kim's hair and pressed the side of her face against the cold, filthy tile on the wall. She leaned in close enough to smell her stale breath. "If you even think of fixing your lips to call me a bitch again... I swear to God that will be the last thing you ever say."

Kim wasn't aggressive at all, so she never attempted to fight back, but as soon as Priscilla loosened her grip, a straight edge razor grazed the bottom of her chin.

She jumped back, grabbed at her face and Kim swung the flat, rectangular blade again leaving a two inch gash across Priscilla's arm.

She stood there, smiling, holding the razor.

"Bitch!"

Priscilla caught a glimpse of her face in the mirror and then she looked at the blood dripping down her hand and thought twice about her next move.

"This shit a'int over, bitch." She whispered, snatched some paper towels, wrapped her bloody arm up and went back to her cot.

Her first day of re-entry into the world had proved to be by far one of the worst days of her life, and yet, she still had so much to go through in order to fulfill her plan.

She tried to not go to sleep, but the weight of her lids felt like a bag of bricks and the next time she opened her eyes it was fourteen hours later.

Priscilla looked up and noticed that she was no longer in a dorm, this was somebody's room.

The walls were painted a yellowish/orange color which made the sun's illuminating rays even more glaring and despite the warm temperatures, a cool breeze flowed through the huge bay window that overlooked the yard.

Priscilla lay staring up at the old ceiling fan, watching the wooden blades go round and round.

"You finally woke up, huh?" The woman's voice sounded familiar, but Priscilla couldn't see too clearly. She lifted her head, squinted and tried to make out who this person was coming through the door. "You done got yourself mixed up in something already." She said, shaking her head.

When she finally came closer, Priscilla recognized the woman from the front desk of the shelter.

"Where am I?" She questioned.

"You're still here at the shelter, but you're in my room." The woman placed two aspirins and a glass of water on the table next to the bed. "I found you passed out this morning when I made my round through the dormitory... must'a lost too much blood. Poor baby, you were almost dead. Good thing the nurse got here on time this morning. I don't know what I would have done without her help."

Priscilla coughed and her head felt like it was about to explode. "Owww... my head is pounding." She looked at her hand and instead of the paper towels she used; it was now wrapped in a real bandage made of gauze. "How bad is it?"

"Not too bad... here, take these and lay back down." She handed Priscilla the aspirins and the water. "That scar on your face there, may be a lifetime memory."

Priscilla had forgotten about getting cut on her face. She couldn't feel a thing. "My face?" she panicked and reached for her cheek.

"No, don't touch it." The woman grabbed her arm. "You'll jus' make it bleed again. Nurse Betty had to stitch you up real good. You got seven on your face and five more on that arm. You wanna talk about it?"

Priscilla shook her head no, and lay back in the warm bed. She shut her eyes and a vision of Brandi made her spring right back up. "My baby!" she pushed the covers off and attempted make an exit, but the loss of blood debilitated her completely. She was too weak to hold her body weight and collapsed to the floor.

"Girl, you gon' kill yourself, now stop being so hardheaded and let me help you up." The woman assisted in getting Priscilla back into the bed. "Now, aint nobody said you got to stay here, if you wanna leave, you know exactly where that door is, but think about it first."

"I need to get my daughter back, please..." Priscilla complained.

"Okay, listen... there are rules that everyone abides by in here. First off let me start by saying, everyone here calls me Ms. Kathy. Like I told you before, I was once in the same exact spot you're in now." Kathy took a seat on the bed next to Priscilla. "Anyway... the rules as stated are; curfew begins today. That means you're in this house by seven-thirty pm every night for the next thirty days. No exceptions. Next, no outside company at all; third, for the first ten days you are on a probation period which means you do not leave the house unless you are told to; fourth, you will participate in household chores. Every morning you will be assigned a task for the day. Failure to complete that task will result in disciplinary actions and last but not least, absolutely *no* drug use whatsoever. Are we clear Ms. Davis?"

"Ten days?" Priscilla couldn't get past not leaving the house.

"Yes, ten days. Do you have a problem with that?"

"Yes, I do because I need to find my daughter." She felt the puddle about to overflow from her eyelids.

"Where is she?"

A river of tears rushed down Priscilla's face. "I… I don't know…" she sobbed, uncontrollably.

Kathy rubbed Priscilla's shoulder. "Well, I wanna help you, so tell me everything that happened…"

CHAPTER FIVE

The dazzling array of colors and continuous explosions lit the warm ebony sky on the evening of July 4th while the smell of gun powder lurked loosely in the air for a few miles.

A group of junior high school kids raced up and down the strip with book bags and matches, lighting fireworks; each time almost blowing their little fingers to oblivion.

It was the day of independence. Our independence, and it was a day when families put aside differences and came together to share laughs, food and fond memories. Generations of cousins, uncles, aunts, nieces and nephews, all who share the same bloodline, united on this day in celebration.

In the park, directly across from building 60, Tyrell sat atop a bench in a grey tank top, blue, Nautica beach shorts and a pair of white, Air Force Ones. He was fresh and he was in power.

He split the Dutch Master he was holding down the middle, dumped the guts in the grass, sprinkled the green buds into the cigar and rolled it.

When he reached for his lighter, it wasn't in his pocket so he went to ask one of the kids lighting the fireworks, but from the corner of his eye he could see someone coming up the walkway.

"What's good, O.G? Lemme get some fire from you?" When the dark figure stepped closer to the light, Tyrell immediately recognized who it was. "Oh shit, Uncle Wise, wassup wit' you?"

"Ain't nothin' good, yougin'" Earl went into his pocket and handed Tyrell a lighter. "Jus' left that damn hospital..." He said, shaking his head.

Tyrell lit the blunt and took a long drag. "Oh, word... how that go?"

"It's sad man... shit is real sad." Earl took a seat on the bench next to Tyrell. "Jus' the fact that I got to sit there and see my nephew suffer so much and ain't shit I could do about it." He pulled a cigarette from his pack and lit it. "I mean... I ain't never saw Mox in a position where he was down... never. Ever since he came up, he stayed at the top. He's a winner, man and to see him all bandaged up like that and his face all fucked up... that's some crazy shit. Feel me? The nigga ain't responsive, he ain't giving nobody no signs... I don't know man... I'm praying for the best, but prepared for the worse. Ya dig?"

In between smoking and listening to Earl, Tyrell was serving his customers. "Hol' up. Unc." He turned to the female that stood impatiently waiting by the gate. "How many you want?"

The shoddy female with a scarf tied around her head flashed ten fingers and approached the bench. "I'ma dollar short... I got forty-nine." She passed him two crumpled twenty dollar bills and nine singles.

Tyrell looked to see if it was clear, reached in his pocket and pulled out a zip-lock baggie full of crack. He counted out ten pieces and handed them to the female. "I want my dollar when you come back."

"You know I spends money, nephew... I got you." She said, skipping away.

Tyrell faced Earl. “Mox is a strong dude, I know he gon’ pull through.” He stuffed the money in his pocket.

“Yeah, I hope so.” Earl replied. “You getting’ money out here, huh?” he questioned.

Tyrell blew the smoke through his nostrils. “Yeah, you see me. I got this shit in the chokehold.” He pulled the baggie from his pocket. “Look at these shits... these is nicks, them niggas over there selling dimes and they shit aint half the size of these.” He dumped a few in Earl’s hand.

After he took a drag of his Newport, Earl grinned because he knew quality work just by looking at it and what Tyrell had was top of the line cook-up. “How you able to do this?”

“I got a sweet connect.”

Earl studied the small, white rocks. “You cookin’ it yourself?”

“Yup... they call me ‘Chef Boy R’...” he laughed. “Why you wanna know anyway, Unc... you don’t fuck with this shit.”

“Sure don’t.” Earl gave the rocks back. “But I’ll tell you this... you sittin’ out here on this bench wit’ a pocket full a’ stones and a stack a’ cash, smoking weed and slangin’ like it’s legal... fuck is wrong wit’ you?”

Tyrell lit his blunt after it went out. “I’m hungry, Unc... gotta get this bread, but shit aint pumpin’ like I thought it would.”

"You *hungry?"* Earl stood up. "When hungry niggas see food they eat. You can't tell me you don't see this goddamn plate in front of yo' face... you hungry ain't you nigga?" Tyrell nodded his head, yes. "Well... eat!"

"I'm out here. You see me eatin' it." He inhaled the smoke.

Earl slowly shook his head. "Nah, yougin' you jus' nibblin' off the plate right now. It's *real* money out here and you playin' games."

"Shiitt..." Tyrell stood up. "You mus' got me confused old man," he raised his tank top and exposed his two guns. "we don't play games over here."

Earl smiled and then chuckled. "Nigga, you got guns too? You must'a bumped yo' goddanm head boy."

"Shit real out here, Earl." Tyrell pulled one of the guns off his waist and cocked it. "If a nigga think he comin' up in here to take mines," he aimed the weapon at a glass bottle that sat on the stone wall about forty feet away. "He got it fucked up." The gun ruptured, blew the glass bottle to shreds and nobody even turned their head. The sound of the shot was hidden in the fireworks.

Earl could do nothing but shake his head. "You need guidance youngin'... let me tell you something." He plucked his cigarette. "I made Mox a whole lotta money out here. Ironically, from these same benches we standin' in front of right now. When that car wash shit popped off, that nigga was gettin' so much work he didn't know what to do wit' it... mind you, prior to this, Mox aint never sold a drug a day in his life, but it was in his blood; he jus' didn't know it. He use' to call me and be like, meet me in the back Unc, so I go back there and the nigga hand me a shopping bag wit' a sneaker box in it." He pulled another cigarette from his pack and lit it. "I take the bag upstairs, crack the box open and it's two fuckin' keys in that bitch."

Tyrell knew Mox was getting money, but he had no idea he was doing it like that. "Word?"

"No bullshit. I had my young wolves out here... you remember Damion and Daren right?"

"Hell yeah... the Wolf brothers, what happened to them dudes?" Tyrell asked.

"They was down for a second on a attempted murder rap, but new evidence jus' came forth and they got released today. My boys be up here tomorrow night." Earl sucked in the smoke and let it filter through his nostrils. "What I'm sayin' is... you need a team out here. If you organize this shit right, you can make millions... I'm tellin' you. Fuck wit' me... I'll make you rich."

Tyrell was skeptical on accepting Earl's advance because he was mindful of his track record, but he did know for a fact that Uncle Wise was a certified hustler.

His eyes went to Earl's arms. "You still fuckin' around?" he could see the track marks coming down from his biceps.

Earl was embarrassed. "Look at me, youngin'..." he held his trembling hands out in front of him. "I'm sick. I ain't did nothin' since the night before Mox got hit."

"I don't know, Unc... I don't think I could trust you."

"That's cool... shit, I wouldn't trust me either, but it ain't about trust, yougin. It's about respect and being real wit' each other. If I can't do something I'ma let you know I can't do it and I expect the same from you, but at the same time, I put my all into whatever it is I get involved with. I can guarantee you one hundred and fifty percent on my end... We can debate about this all day, but there's only one way to find out..." Earl dapped the youngster and walked out of the park. "I'ma see you tomorrow."

Tyrell thought about everything Earl spoke on and came to the conclusion that he was right. Without a team there was no way he could expand and take his hustle to the next level. He needed manpower and Wise Earl was going to provide that.

Since his homeboy Leo went down for the murder, the only person he dealt with on a level of that caliber was his other childhood friend, Six.

Corey Bellows aka Six is a 17 year old, 6 foot 2 inch high school dropout with a golden bronze skin complexion, short, coarse hair that's always uncombed, peasy and dry, and to add to that, he has a missing front tooth that gives him a distinctive, menacing appeal.

He and Tyrell lived on separate sides of town and went to different schools, but became good friends as kids when they played pop warner football together.

Corey was always into his books, so a lot of his peers would shy away from him and most times, view him as a nerd, but Tyrell took a liking to him. He was conscious of Corey's knowledge and truly appreciative of his friendship. The two of them had been comrades for more than eight years.

Born on the west side of New Rochelle, Corey lived with his mother, father and baby sister in a one family, three bedroom house, on Third Street. His mother worked in Pelham as a home health aide five days a week and his father drove city busses for the Westechester Bee-line Bus Company.

Up until last year, Corey had lived the life of the typical teenager, raised by strict, middle class parents, but everything changed on the night of his sixteenth birthday.

It was 2:30 am when Corey strolled into the silent, dark house, hungry and a bit tipsy. He had just come in from a get together that one of his friends arranged for him and he could no longer take the pain and growling of his stomach, so he opted to fix himself a grilled cheese sandwich before he went to sleep.

While he waited for his food to finish, all the water he had been drinking to sober up was ready to come out, so he went to use the bathroom.

He figured by the time he came out, the sandwich would be done, but the only problem was, after he relaxed on the cushioned toilet seat, his eyelids started to put on weight and he soon drifted into a deep, soundless sleep, sitting on the porcelain chair.

When Corey woke up his arms and legs were wrapped in bandages, he was lying in a hospital bed and a doctor was standing directly over him.

He looked up at the pale Caucasian male and asked. "Where am I?"

"In the hospital." The doctor replied.

"*Hospital*... why?" He had no recollection or idea of the previous events.

"There was an accident."

Corey tried to sit upright. "*Accident?*" he looked around. "Where are my parents?"

The doctor shook his head. He disfavored being the person who had to break the bad news to people, especially young kids. "I'm sorry son... they didn't make it..."

The news headline read: **TEEN SETS HOUSE ABLAZE WHILE PARENTS SLEEP**

Corey got charged with two counts of first degree murder and was forced to fight his case from the inside prison. He sat in the county jail unable to make bail for more than a year, awaiting a trial that only lasted two weeks, but the end result was not guilty. He had just been released two days ago.

"Whaddup, homey?" Six approached the benches, extended his hand and dapped Tyrell.

He was shirtless, showing off his new chiseled frame and all the tattoos that covered his upper body. His off white, True Religion beach shorts sagged slightly off his 36inch waist and he let the strings hang on his crispy, pearl white Nike Foamposites.

"Six, what's good?" Tyrell responded.

"Aint shit," he took a seat on the bench. "Yo, you know what's crazy?"

"What's that?"

"Most people in the hood don't even know what the fourth of July represents. They jus' be happy to see some fireworks and eat a few burgers n' shit." Six laughed and then pulled a cigar from his pocket, split it and let the guts fall to the concrete.

"I guess I'm most people then..." Tryell smirked. "I mean... I know it got somethin' to do with the Great Britain and the declaration of independence n' shit, but that's about it."

"Honestly, as black people we shouldn't even be celebrating this shit because the reality of it is... we weren't free then and we're still not free now."

Tyrell nodded in agreement. "You right about that."

"Fuck the fourth of July... lemme get a light." Six lit the blunt and took a deep pull. "So, wassup... it's slow out here today?"

"Nah, it's moving. I ran through half a pack already."

"Okay... yo, I jus' seen that funny lookin' nigga Gahbe on the block... he stuntin' hard too."

"Fuck Gahbe!" Tyrell got tight and screwed his face up. "Old ass nigga... I'm tellin' you son, if I catch one of them niggas in here makin' a chop; I'm poppin' on 'em... I aint got no words for niggas."

"Damn, son... it's like that?"

"Yo," Tyrell hopped of the bench and stood directly in front of Six. "Look at me my nigga..." he flashed the two weapons on his waist. "I don't fuck wit' that nigga Gahbe at all. That bitchassnigga is the reason my moms is fucked up on this crack shit now... I'm tellin' you Six," he clenched his jaws. "If any one of them niggas step foot in here, my shit going off."

Six stared at him. "Yo, you wildin' my nigga."

"Nah, I aint wildin'... we bout to get rich nigga." Tyrell eyed Six. "I don't know, Six... you was talking alotta G' shit when you was locked up... it's time nigga."

"Time for what?"

Tyrell smiled, pulled a gun from his waistline and tossed it to Six. "Time to put that work in nigga."

CHAPTER SIX

An entire month had gone by and Priscilla was beginning to settle into the shelter. On the count of this being the only place she had to go, she put aside her pride and focused on getting her life together.

At all cost she avoided any type of drama that would deter her from completing her goals. A few times she even had to hold her tongue.

After three weeks of job searching, Priscilla was ready to give up on the hunt and figure out a second alternative to appease her financial woes. It was stressful and the irksome interviewing process was starting to wear on her conscience and deplete her self-esteem. But just when she was ready to throw the towel in, a call came from an employer.

"Priscilla, hurry up." Ms. Kathy was holding the phone. She whispered. "I think it's a job."

Priscilla rushed out of the dorm and grabbed the cordless. "Hello?"

"Hello, Ms. Davis... this is Catherine Welch, hiring manager at Stop & Shop supermarket. How are you doing today?"

"Fine, thank you." She replied.

"Well, I'm calling because we've looked over your application and I've also spoken with Jim, who you did the interview with... and we would like to know if you're still interested in working here and if so, when can you start?"

Priscilla's eyes lit up and a smile widened her face for the first time in a while. "Ughh..." she was so excited she couldn't speak. "Ummm.. yeah, I'm very much interested. I can start tomorrow if you want me to."

Ms. Welch loved Priscilla's enthusiasm. "Great, but since tomorrow is Sunday; how about you come in at nine am on Monday and we can take care of the paperwork?"

"Monday sounds great... see you at nine... and thank you."

Ms. Welch said bye and hung the phone up on her end. Priscilla was caught in a befuddled shock, she didn't realize that she was still holding the phone to her ear, but no one was on the other end.

"Well," Ms. Kathy held out her hands waiting for a response. "What happened?"

Priscilla stayed silent for a few seconds, blinked her eyes and then placed the phone on the front desk. "I got the job..." she still couldn't believe it. "I got the job, Ms. Kathy!" she yelled.

"Yey!" Ms. Kathy hugged her because she was proud of her accomplishment.

She had witnessed the strain and struggle Priscilla had been going through and coming from a similar place, she could sympathize with why she would sometimes act out the way she did.

So, for the past week Priscilla had been getting out of bed at 6:30 am, taking a shower, eating breakfast and heading out to Mount Vernon so she could punch the clock by 7:30.

For the first time in her life, she had a job. It may not have been the job she wanted, but she was definitely grateful and accepting of the blessing.

Even on the mornings that she didn't want to get up, God gave her the strength to spring from the bed, put a smile on her face and make the best of the day.

She was determined.

She was eager.

For eight hours a day, Priscilla watched as the cashiers scanned barcodes, requested price checks and handled money. In a way, it reminded her of the days when she was hustling drugs, but she immediately washed those thoughts from her mental and maintained focus. Once she learned the ins and outs of the checkout area, she quickly devised a plan to make things run faster. The results of a faster moving line would be more tips.

For two days straight, she watched the cashiers at each checkout line to see who was processing the customer's items the fastest. When she figured out who it was, she approached him.

"Hey Randy," Priscilla closed her line and made her way toward the frail white kid working at the register next to her. "Did you take your break yet?"

Randy thought about it. "Nope, this line been crazy today... I'm ready to."

"Well, c'mon... I need to talk to you about something." Priscilla threw the charm on thick. "I got this sandwich too..." she held up a bag. "I know I'm not gonna eat the whole thing so you can save your money and take the other half of this."

"What kind is it?"

"Ham and cheese."

Randy licked his lips and smiled. "Oh yeah, that's my favorite."

He may have believed it was just a coincidence, but Priscilla knew otherwise. She had been doing her scouting work and overheard him mention his love for ham sandwiches while they stood out front on break.

Randy took care of the last two customers on his line, flicked the 'closed' switch and hurried out to the front.

"So, what is it that you wanna talk about?" he said, holding the half sandwich in his hand. He took a bite and some mayonnaise got stuck on the side of his mouth.

"I know I only been here a few days, but I been watching you on that register and you be moving." Priscilla tapped him on the side of his arm.

He tried to reply but he had a mouth full of food. "Excuse me… I don't mean to toot my own horn…" he took another bite. "But, I am the fastest cashier on the day shift." Particles of bread, meat and cheese flew from his mouth.

"I know; that's what I'm sayin'…" She was stroking his ego, but at the same time, he *was* the fastest cashier. "So, how does that work, do you get to choose your baggers?"

Randy stopped eating for a minute. "Well, since I am top dog, I get to choose who I want on my line."

"Is that right?"

He grinned. "Yup."

"So why is it that you have the slowest bagger in the store at your register?"

"Oh, Tara?" He cheesed. "I know she's slow, but she's pretty and I like her."

"But if you had a faster bagger you could make more in tips; how much are y'all gettin' now?"

Randy scratched his head. "On a good weekday, maybe twenty dollars; on the weekend, twenty-five or thirty."

"That's it? Man, we over here pullin' in at least fifty dollars a night... and that's a regular night. Let's not even discuss the weekend."

"Fifty dollars!? Stop lying." he couldn't believe it.

Priscilla made a cross on her chest with her fingers, kissed her palm and raised her right hand to the sky. "All truth."

"Okay... cool, but let me ask you something?" he said.

"I'm listenin'."

Randy finished the half sandwich and tossed the bag in the garbage. "You shared your delicious lunch with me and brought me out here to tell me that I'm the fastest cashier or is there something else?"

"Actually, there is..." Her voice got low. "If me and you were a team in there, we could make a lot of extra money. Think about it, a whole twenty-five extra dollars a day in your pocket, sometimes even more."

Randy contemplated. "I don't know Priscilla... what about Tara?"

"What about her?" Priscilla moved in closer. "Randy; you and Tara been working here together for how long?"

"Almost six months."

"In that time has she ever greeted you, smiled at you, or even looked your way?"

He thought about it. "Ummm... not really."

"See, that's what I mean... Tara's not worthy of you Randy, you're handsome, smart and independent. I'm sure there's plenty of girls out here waiting for a guy like you to come scoop them off their feet."

He blushed. "You think I'm handsome?"

"Of course I do... now, I want you to go in there and tell Tara that she's no longer bagging at register eleven... show her you're the man, Randy." Priscilla was trying her best not to laugh.

"On one condition." He pointed to the bag in her hand.

"This?" she held up the bag. "But what will I eat for lunch?"

Randy shrugged his shoulders. "Hey, you wanna bag at my register... hand over the sandwich."

Priscilla threw on a fake expression of sadness and passed the bag to Randy. The truth was, she had never eaten pork in her life.

When they went back inside, Randy walked right up to Tara and made it clear that she would no longer be bagging at his register. She got upset and threw a slight tantrum until Priscilla checked her.

"Listen, bitch... take yo' lil' skinny ass down there somewhere and bag groceries. I got this now."

Her first move had been made.

Priscilla worked strenuously every day and raked in hundreds of dollars in tips throughout the week that she tucked away in her stash. The only way she could make anything happen was to have some money.

On the job, she never bothered to make any new friends; she kept quiet and extracted herself from the daily doings of her fellow employees.

She was in her own world.

At 4:30 every afternoon she would punch out, grab something to eat and hop on the number 42 bus back to New Rochelle and every day on her stroll back to the shelter, Priscilla would wince at the grim site of the hospital that housed her love, but on this day that little voice in her head would get the best of her.

When the bus doors came open the splatter, of the torrential rains sprinkled Priscilla's cheeks before she could lift her umbrella.

"Be safe Ms. Davis... have a good night." Tom the bus driver said.

She stepped into the wet streets and looked up at the overclouded, dark grey skies and that's when she heard it.

Priscilla...

She looked around, but the only things moving were the cars traveling up and down the roads.

Priscilla...

She heard it again, this time she thought she recognized the voice. It sounded like Mox.

Priscilla turned her head and her eyes fell on the hospital.

She hadn't seen Mox since the day she returned home and her last visual recollection of him was not a pleasant one. It had been a frightening situation that continuously replayed in her brain every time she thought about him.

It was time for her to make a decision.

It was time for her to face the fear.

Without a second thought, she made her move. In the blink of an eye, Priscilla was walking through the automatic doors to the entrance of the hospital.

The cool air sent a chill through her body as soon as she stepped into the lobby entrance. She shook the excess rain from her umbrella, wrapped it up and brushed her wet shoes on the carpet. When she got to the information desk, a young, short haired, brown eyed blonde girl with a pair of specs sat behind the glass.

She smiled and said. "Welcome to Sound Shore, how can I help you today?"

Priscilla looked around. She never really cared for hospitals. They made her feel sick. "Yes, I'm trying to visit my friend... his name is Mox Daniels."

The blonde nodded her head and proceeded to tap the keys on the keyboard in front of her. "Yes... Mr. Daniels has been moved from the third floor to the second floor, which is a good thing." She said, as she continued typing. "Oh, I see it right here... he's in room 207. That's the second floor, when you get off the elevator you make the right." She slid Priscilla a nametag and a pen. "Write your name on that and keep it with you."

When the elevator door opened, Priscilla slowly stepped out and made the first right as directed. After a brief thought about what she was doing; she felt a slight shift in the pit of her stomach and perspiration began to build on her brow and under her armpits.

She used the back of her hand to wipe her forehead and when she looked up, room 207 was directly in front of her.

If she hesitated, there was a chance for her to turn on her heels and walk away, so she grabbed the knob and gently pushed the door open.

"Oh, excuse me... I'm just finishing up here. I should be done in a sec."

The first thing Priscilla noticed was that the woman standing next to Mox's bed, wearing nurse scrubs, was pretty as hell.

She was short, maybe 5 feet 4 inches with brown shoulder length hair, a golden, bronzed complexion and a nice petite shaped body.

"Is he awake?" Priscilla took a step closer.

The nurse removed her gloves. "I'm sorry... Ms.??"

"Ms. Davis." Priscilla extended her hand.

"How are you? I'm Jasmine. I've been Mr. Daniels' nurse for the past few weeks... ummm... Miss Davis... Mr. Daniels hasn't been awake since he's been admitted."

Priscilla stared at Mox lying on the hospital bed. It was an unpleasant sight. In all her days of knowing him, he had never looked so overthrown, so worn out and so powerless.

She struggled to repress the tears, but the weight of her emotions was too much to bear and her eyes could no longer contain the waterfall.

Jasmine could see the grief plastered all over Priscilla's face; she could sense the love in the room. "I'll leave you two alone for a minute." she fixed the sheet that was covering Mox and left.

Besides the beeping of the machines and the slight sound of his breathing, the room held an awkward quietness that sent a chill through Priscilla's spine.

She eyed the motionless figure lying before her. "Mox." she whispered.

His skin looked dry and discolored from lack of vitamins and moisturizer and it was obvious he had lost a few pounds over the weeks. “Baby I’m here...” droplets spewed from her eyes.

She placed her hand on top of his.

His skin was dry and rough.

He made no indication of response.

He just lay there, eyes closed, taking short breaths.

Priscilla squeezed his hand. “Baby wake up...” she sobbed. “Mox don’t do this... I need you, Brandi needs you.”

Vivid images of past memories flashed before Priscilla’s eyes.

The first time they met.

Their first kiss.

The first time they made love.

And then Brandi’s bright smile appeared and Priscilla felt her spirit being whisked away.

The pouring rains tapped against the second floor widows and Priscilla’s cries grew louder causing her tears to fall faster. “Pleeeeeaaase don’t leave me Mox...” She bent down, pulled her shoes off and got into the hospital bed beside him. “Mox...” she brushed his face with her hand. “Baby, you gotta be strong, you gotta fight Mox.” she laid her head on his chest and for a second it reminded her of the past times they shared.

Priscilla closed her eyes, got in as close as she could and wrapped her arm around his torso. "You gotta fight baby..."

Lying in that bed next to the only man who had ever cared for her enabled Priscilla to realize how beloved a life really is and how much she had taken the small things for granted.

She thought about her mother.

Her daughter.

Mox.

And herself.

For Priscilla, this was a test; a test of her strength, will and courage; a test to see if she really could get beyond her disturbing past experiences and devote her every minute to building a solid, communicable relationship; a test to see if she could open her heart and truly love another human being; a test of her diligence; a test of her faith.

Staring at the ceiling, she made a promise; a troth, to herself and to Mox that from this day on she would stand by his side until he was able to fully recover and return to his normal state. Meanwhile, she would do anything in her power to find Brandi's whereabouts and get her back.

It was time for Priscilla to throw her game face on and turn the heat up in the kitchen... It was time for her to make a return.

CHAPTER SEVEN

The music played at a moderate level as the drinks flowed and cries of laughter filled the atmosphere in Vito's Bar & Grill. The Partygoers mingled amongst themselves in celebration of Billy Telesco's return home from a four and a half year prison bid for an assault charge.

Mikey stood at the center of the dining area, raised his glass of champagne and yelled. "Felicitazioni!" (Congrats!) and the entire room followed suit.

Billy Telesco aka 'The Butcher' was Vinny's oldest nephew and had been labeled a certified knuckle head by his longtime peers. He earned his nickname, 'The Butcher' as a hard boiled teen who never took kindly to the word 'no' and honestly loved the sight of blood.

As a youth, Billy was into stick-ups and friendly extortion as he rose to power on his way to becoming a made man. His lanky figure and brash demeanor could never go unnoticed when he entered a room and those that knew him well, kept their distance.

Five years ago on a foggy September evening in Queens Village NY, twenty-four year old Billy 'The Butcher' and twenty-one year old Mikey T strutted into the Silver Moon Diner at 23520 Hillside Avenue. They were hungry, tired and fed up with how the day's events had played out. All they wanted was a hot meal and a few stiff drinks.

"I'm tellin' ya' Mikey, I should'a wacked his fuckin' ass when I had the chance." Billy was heated. He was dressed in his usual designer, slim fit, metallic Valentino suit, shiny black shoes and dark shades.

They pulled chairs from under the table and sat down.

Mikey replied. "Naw, if you would have done that, then you really wouldn't have gotten paid. I think he got the message."

A waiter approached the duo. "Welcome to the Silver Moon, my name is Dick and I'll be your waiter this evening." He placed two menus on the table. "Can I get you guys something to drink?"

Billy chuckled. "Yeah Dick." He laughed again. "Bring us a bottle of that expensive French shit y'all got back there."

Dick pulled a small drink menu from his pocket. "Will it be the Chateau Lafite, Marguax or the Haut Brion?"

Billy's smile turned to a serious scowl. "Now do I look like I know what the fuck that is? Pick one... now beat it... Dick!" he pounded his fist on the table in amusement.

The waiter turned his lip, sucked his teeth and pranced off in a fit.

"Be nice Billy..." Mikey giggled.

After forty minutes at the table, Mikey was stuffed and Billy was tipsy, due to finishing half the bottle of wine by himself.

"Hey, I gotta take a whizz." Billy got up, walked through the dining area, down a short corridor and into the men's restroom.

On his way out, he thought he saw a familiar face, but he didn't stop until he got back to the table. "Mikey, doesn't that look like that fuckin' scumbag, Jimmy Rovelli over there?"

Mikey tried not to be obvious and glanced over. "Yup, that's him."

"I knew it!" Billy downed the rest of the wine in his glass and wiped his mouth with a handkerchief. "Lemme see your gun Mikey."

"I left it in the car."

"You left it in the *car??* What the fuck Mikey... fuck it." He stormed off toward the kitchen, and when he returned, Mikey caught a glimpse of the ten inch carbon steel blade he was gripping.

He tried to stop him, but it was too late.

"Hey, Jimmy... lemme talk to you for a second." Billy forced a fake smile and held the steak knife at his side.

Hey, Billy... what's goin' on? I know you didn't jus' come from the kitchen, you workin' here now?" he smirked. He acted nonchalant, but Jimmy knew exactly what Billy wanted to talk about.

Billy matched his smirk. "Yeah... somethin' like that. Hey... where's that ten large you owe me?"

Jimmy's chipper expression turned to a glower. "C'mon, Billy this is not the place or the time to discuss this; we both know that."

Billy looked at Mikey and then clenched the knife tighter. "Jimmy... you must think 'cause you wake up every mornin' and slip into your little blue suit that you garner some type of authority or somethin'."

Jimmy looked down and saw the knife in his hand. "Billy, don't do it. You know you can't get away with this."

"Who said I gave a fuck about gettin' away." He reached out, snatched Jimmy by his collar and put the blade to his throat.

Jimmy's wife scurried to his side. "Please don't hurt him."

"Bitch, shut up!" he pressed the stainless steel harder into Jimmy's neck. "Mikey, c'mere."

A nervous Mikey T wanted to hesitate, but he knew better, so he hurried over to where Billy was.

The other three couples that were sitting at their respective tables, dining, pushed their food to the side and rushed for the door.

Mikey got in close on Billy's ear. "You know this guy's a fuckin' cop right?"

Billy displayed his thirty-two's. "I know..." he whispered. "That makes it allll the better."

"Billy, please... gimme a week." Saliva slid down the side of Jimmy's mouth.

"You been dippin' n dodgin' me for two months, Jimmy. It's the principles." He laughed.

Jimmy begged. "Pleeeaaasee."

"Mikey... grab his hand."

Jimmy's wife was screaming at the top of her lungs.

Mikey snatched Jimmy's arm and slammed his hand on the table.

"The pinky Mikey... I want the pinky."

"Please... no!" Jimmy wailed.

Billy sneered at Mrs. Rovelli. "Next time, it'll be his dick!"

He raised the knife and smashed it down on Jimmy's pinky finger.

"Ahhhhhhhh!!"

You could hear the splitting of the bone on contact.

Blood shot from the wound and sprinkled Billy's expensive suit. "Shit!" he jumped back and attempted to wipe the stain, but only smeared it. "You muthafucka!" he lifted the blade and went to strike Jimmy a second time, but Mikey grabbed his arm.

"That's enough, Billy!"

Mrs. Rovelli snatched a handkerchief, wrapped it around her husband's bleeding hand and pulled out her cell phone. "I'm calling the cops, Jimmy!"

"Gimme that goddamn phone." Billy snatched it from her hand and flung it into the closest wall, shattering it to pieces. He looked down at Jimmy's severed finger and smiled. "You'll get this back when I get my money." and he tossed the bloody extremity into his pocket and walked out.

On the grounds of Billy being a made guy, the department made a deal with the Telesco's that would exonerate Mikey of all charges and induce the minimum sentence of four years on Billy; and those four years flew by.

"Great to see you back home kid," Vinny hugged his nephew and kissed the sides of his cheeks.

"Good to see you too, Unc... but I'm still pissed about missing Vito's funeral."

Vinny grabbed the young Mafioso by the shoulder and led him through the crowd towards the bar. "Don't get your nuts in a bunch over it... some things we have no control over... excuse me..." Vinny put his hand to his mouth and coughed. "Tonight we celebrate your freedom. Hey, Tony... get me that envelope I gave to you earlier."

Tony reached under the bar and slid a manila envelope down to Vinny.

"What's this?" Billy shook the envelope when Vinny handed it to him.

"That's what it's about now Billy, get as much of it as you could."

Billy stuck his hand in the envelope and pulled the stack of fifty's from it. "Thanks Uncle Vinny."

"No problem, make sure you get laid tonight and call me in the morning. I got a job for you."

Billy smiled and began counting the bills in his hand when Mikey walked over. "You ready to get ya' balls out the sand?" he gestured to a tall brunette with huge tits and a slim waist that was standing about thirty feet away.

Billy licked his lips. "It's been long enough Mikey!"

The bells on the front door jingled and when Billy looked up the face staring back at him was one he sure didn't expect to see.

"Billy Telesco... You still look the same." Jimmy said, walking in with his partner.

Over the years, he had put on a few pounds, so Billy didn't recognize him at first glance. He removed the shades from his face and walked to the bar.

"You got some fuckin' nerve showin' up here, Jimmy." Billy got off the stool he was sitting on and shot him an ice grill.

"Now, now Billy... don't you think it's been long enough? I mean... I've forgiven you." Jimmy smirked. "I see you're still wearing those cheap ass suits."

"Fuck you."

"Did he just say fuck *me*?" Jimmy pointed at himself and then looked to his partner. "Naw, I think *you're* the one that's been gettin' fucked little Billy. Hey, I heard you got butter fingers... how many times you drop the soap!?" he and his partner broke out in a boisterous laughter.

Billy reached out, snatched Jimmy by his throat and whipped a steel handled blade out the inside pocket of his suit jacket.

Jimmy's partner unlatched the weapon on his waistline and drew it on Billy.

"Grab his hand Mikey!"

Mikey froze.

"Put the weapon down!" The officer warned.

"Mikey! Grab his fuckin' hand!"

Jimmy tried to speak, but Billy tightened his grip.

"Drop the fucking knife!" His hand was shaking. This was the first time he ever had to draw his gun on a civilian.

Billy shifted his attention to the officer. "If you was gon' shoot, you would'a done it already... fuckin' rookie." his focus went back to Jimmy. "This time I'ma cut ya' fuckin' dick off!"

"Hey! Hey!" Vinny pushed his way through the crowd. "Jimmy! Put the goddamn knife down and let 'em go."

"But, Unc..."

Vinny's eyes got beady and his temper flared, his old age was beginning to get the best of him. "Don't fuckin' but me Billy... jus' do what I say." He covered his mouth and coughed hard.

Billy slowly put the blade away and loosened his grip on Jimmy's neck. "You're lucky... fuckin' prick." He looked down at the badge on his chest and spit on it. "Fuck the boys in blue..."

Jimmy's partner went to grab Billy's arm, but a straight left hand landed on the tip of his nose and his top lip.

The rookie stumbled back, touched his nose and blood started to drip down his hand. "You bastard!" he grumbled and went to charge at Billy.

"C'mon muthafucka!" Billy flashed the knife again, but this time he was going to use it.

Mikey stepped between the two men. "Not here, Billy." he put his arm around him and they walked to the back.

Jimmy was wiping the saliva off his badge. "You going back to jail Billy!" he shouted.

"Nobody's going anywhere." Vinny tossed a clean handkerchief to the bleeding rookie. "Clean yourself up." he turned to Jimmy. "You had no fuckin' right comin' here in the first place, you work in the city... what the hell you doin' in Westchester County?"

"No disrespect Vinny, but..."

Vinny cut him off. "Get the fuck outta my restaurant..."

Jimmy knew better than to challenge Vinny, so he tapped his partner on the shoulder and the two blue suits walked out.

CHAPTER EIGHT

Chris slightly pressed the brakes and then hit the lights on the Town Car as he cruised across the empty street. The dark vehicle merged with the shadowy black night atmosphere, came to a full stop and he parallel parked between a blue work van and a Cadillac truck.

"Is this close enough?" He asked.

Cleo blew the smoke from his cigarette at the roof and then looked down at the chrome lined, wood stock, Romanian AK-47 that sat in his lap. "Yeah, this is good."

He pulled out a pair of black Nike baseball gloves from the back of the front passenger seat, slipped one on his left hand, and then picked up the thirty round magazine that was right next to him. He pressed the cartridge into the weapon and glanced at his reflection in the tinted window.

"I'ma make these muthafuckas pay for what they did to me..." he had fifty-six stiches on the side of his face and his right hand was fully wrapped in a bandage.

Chris looked in the rearview at Cleo. "How long we gotta wait?"

Cleo made a pained expression when he lifted the AK with his injured hand, but he managed to pull the hammer back and a bullet slid into the chamber. "Until I say move." He pressed a button on the door panel and the window slowly came down. "It's nice out here tonight too." a relaxed summer breeze entered the vehicle and kissed his face. "Chris, you ever read *The Art of War* by Sun Tzu?"

"Nah, why you ask?"

Cleo settled back in the seat, grasping the military issued firearm. "When I was back there on that kitchen table at your homeboy's house gettin' stitched up, I thought about a quote I remembered from that book... Sun Tzu said, *in conflict, direct confrontation will lead to engagement and surprise will lead to victory"* Cleo pressed the button and the widow went back up. "If I would'a been thinkin' like that from the start I wouldn't have been on that table..." he brushed the side of the weapon. "This time I got a surprise for dey ass."

An hour and twenty minutes had passed, but Cleo was just as alert as he had been when they pulled up. Besides a passing car every ten minutes, the streets were abandoned and the only establishment open was the Bar & Grill directly across the street from where the Town Car was parked.

Cleo heard what he thought was laughter, so he looked up and saw the door to the Bar & Grill was open and patrons were funneling out.

He tapped Chris on the shoulder, awakening him from his doze. "Chris, wake up... it's time."

"Hey Pop, could you grab my keys for me... I'm gonna drop Billy off to the hotel." Mikey said while he waited by the exit.

Billy pushed the front door open to leave. "Ahh, don't worry about me, Mikey... I'm alright."

"Oh yeah..." Mikey looked down at Billy's feet. "So, why you ain't got no shoes on tough guy?"

Billy dropped his eyes to the cement and burst out in laughter. "Way to go Mikey!" he stumbled out the exit and into the desolate night air.

"Pop, you alright... you need a ride?" Mikey asked.

Vinny swirled the shot of whiskey in his glass, downed it and then ordered another one. “Yeah, I’m okay Mikey… go ahead and get your cousin home safe. I’ll see yous tomorrow.”

“Cool…” Mikey scratched his head trying to think about where he parked his vehicle. “Shit!... hey Billy, where the hell did I park the car?”

Billy was bent down trying to get his shoe onto his foot. “Do I look I know where the fuck you parked, Mikey.”

“Alright, calm down… we’ll find it.”

Partygoers were filing out of the restaurant when a dark colored car with no headlights came barreling down the block.

The roar of the engine made Billy lift his head. “What the fu—”

“I don’t think that’s him Cleo…” Chris hugged the steering wheel and eased off the gas.

“Slow up… slow up.” Cleo let the window come down halfway and then fastened his hand around the weapon. “That’s that muthafucka Billy… I heard he was home, pull up on ‘em.”

Chris hit the gas, sped up and made the tires screech as he came to a full stop right in front of Vito’s Bar & Grill.

"Welcome home Billy!" Cleo yelled and then aimed the high caliber weapon out the window.

He squeezed the trigger and fire shot from the nozzle.

The ear popping sounds of gunshots echoed throughout the vacant streets and the 7.62 caliber bullets pierced flesh and tore away portions of the concrete structures.

Spent shell casings jumped from the flame spitting war gun as Cleo emptied the thirty round magazine at his adversaries.

A bullet struck Billy in the neck before he could attempt to get to the ground and blood shot into the air.

"Billy!!" Mikey watched as his body crumbled to the cement. He reached for his shoulder holster, backed out his chrome, 9 millimeter Beretta and returned blind fire, shattering the windows of parked cars alongside the street, but aimlessly missing his intended target.

An older; married couple, exiting the restaurant walked directly into a shower of stray bullets and were both cut down on contact.

"Pull off Chris!" Cleo tapped the back of the headrest, ducking back into the vehicle.

The nose twitching redolence of burnt rubber and gunpowder mixed with the nauseating, stench of death lingered throughout the air.

"Nooooo!! Billy..." Tears flooded Mikey's eyes as he kneeled beside his first cousin and tried to lift his limp body from the warm ground, but the dead weight was too much for him to manage. When he looked down, his jacket and hands were covered in Billy's blood.

Screaming sirens could be heard in the distance and the sound was moving in closer with each passing second.

Vinny heard the shots from inside and made his way out to the street in a panic. He could barely catch his breath. "Mi... Mikey, you hit?" he coughed and caught a glimpse of the blood spilling out from underneath Billy's body. "Goddamnit Billy..." he reached down and shut his eyes.

Mikey tried to stand up, but his shattered ankle wouldn't allow him to. "I think I took one in the foot, Pop." He slowly lifted his pants leg and saw the red juice covering his shoe; immediately he felt the burn.

"Shit!" Vinny spat. He could see the flashing lights closing in. "Gimme that..." he grabbed the hot pistol from Mikey's hand, stuffed it in his jacket pocket and called to his longtime comrade. "Hey, Sal! Get him outta here."

The lurid display of death was a picturesque scene that mimicked a classic mob flick.

Parked cars riddled with bullets.

Billy Telesco's stiff corpse lolled across the filthy pavement, soaking in a pool of blood. He was in his best suit, most expensive pair of shoes and his Hermes tie was flipped up over his shoulder.

The two innocent bystanders, lying on top of each other, blanketed in blood; were dead at the front entrance of the restaurant.

"Yo, lemme get a pack of Newports and three of those Dutchies." Tyrell slapped a twenty dollar bill onto the counter.

"Ty, you see this shit?" Six was staring at the 15 inch color television affixed to the back wall of the bodega. "Somebody hit the Italians last night...shit crazy."

Tyrell turned and looked up at the local news report on the screen.

I'm standing only fifteen feet away from where the notorious Italian mob gangster, Billy 'The Butcher' Telesco and two others were gunned down late last night in a hail of bullets.

Reports say the victims were leaving a 'welcome home' celebration for the mob affiliate when a dark colored vehicle rolled up to the front of the restaurant and one of its occupants opened fire.

This restaurant, Vito's Bar & Grill, is owned by reputed mob boss, Vinny Telesco, whose youngest son, Vito, was murdered less than a month ago. Vinny Telesco was said to be inside at the time of the shooting and police have yet to identify the other two victims. For more on this story, tune in at 7 pm.

This is Kathy Lee reporting live from White Plains, New York for channel Twelve News.

"Damn... son jus' got home too." Six shook his head.

Tyrell got his change, took his bag off the counter and moved to the exit. "Word... nigga probably didn't even get no ass yet. That's fucked up." he giggled.

In a little over a month's time, Tyrell, with the help of Uncle Earl, assembled a team, flooded the streets with product, and proceeded to make his mark in the drug trade.

His crew consisted of Uncle Earl, the Wolf brothers; (Damion and Daren) and his longtime friend Six.

On average, Tyrell's weekly profits would total 25 to 30 thousand dollars. He controlled the flow of crack cocaine within the gates of the projects and his clientele was growing by the hour.

He now felt the need to expand further into the surrounding area, but he was knowledgeable of the repercussions that would occur with that move, so he prepared himself.

The clouded sky gave off a murky grey tint and a cool September breeze whizzed by, blowing pieces of loose garbage into the street as Tyrell and Six exited the corner store.

A group of seven or eight hustlers were gathered about fifty feet up the block in a detached circle, badgering a short dark skinned kid who was about to roll the dice.

"Watch his face when he ace!" one of the men shouted.

The short dark skinned kid shook the dice in his closed fist and blew on them three times. *"Scared money don't make no money if I ever go broke—"* he unleashed the square ivory cubes from the palm of his hand and they bounced off the wall and rolled across the cement. *"I'ma take yo' money!"* they landed on four, five and six.

"That's some bullshit!!" One of the dicers complained.

"Fuck all that... pay me nigga." He collected his winnings around the circle. *"Twelve hunit comin'... all downs a bet, everything good in my bank, call em' out!"* he bent down and schooled the dice.

Tyrell and his partner were approaching the circle when Six thought he saw Dana crossing the street on the opposite side.

"Ain't that your cousin right there?" He pointed out.

"Yeah, that's her... she ain't fuckin' wit' me right now." he chuckled. "Fuck that tho... I want some of this money." he stepped closer to the circle, pulled out a stack of cash and started flipping through the bills. "What's in the bank?"

Without turning around, the dark skinned kid answered, "It's five hunit left, what you want?"

"I want the whole thing...stop it up."

The words caught dark skin's attention and he turned to see who was speaking. When he acknowledged it was Tyrell, he smiled. "You sure you can cover that lil' nigga?" he grinned.

Tyrell returned the smile. "I can cover anything you put in there... lil' nigga." he dropped the stack of hundred dollar bills on the ground in front of him.

Dark skinned picked the dice back up and went into his routine. "This Gahbe's block nigga!" he raised the dice over his head, gave them a good shaking and then tossed them against the wall. "Show me six, bitches!"

The dice hit the wall and one bounced off someone's shoe. When they stopped, two of them were face up showing the number three, and the last one lay in a crack showing the number one.

Tyrell reached down and picked up his stack of money and the dice. "Three, three, one... nigga, pay me, that's a ace." he said.

But Gahbe was opposed to losing. "Nah, that was in the crack... I aint payin' that."

The hostility in his voice made Six step up and say something. "You ain't bout that life Gahbe, you know bedda than that."

"Who the fuck is you?"

Six answered by pressing the cold steel barrel of his .45 against Gahbe's cheek. "How bad you wanna know?"

Two of the dicers took off running and the few that stayed, were in too much of a shock to move; they just watched.

Tyrell got excited. "That's what the fuck I'm talkin' 'bout, Six! Handle that shit! Boy... I was startin' to wonder about you." he laughed.

"Empty ya' pockets nigga..." Six looked at the other dicers and then waved the gun at them. "All y'all niggas... hurry the fuck up too!"

Gahbe was mumbling something under his breath.

"You said somethin' homie?" Tyrell was close enough to kiss him.

His teeth were clenched, but his words were clear. "Y'all niggas gon' pay for this... word."

Six shoved the gun back in his face. "Shut up nigga... gimmie that watch, gimme that chain... oh," he looked at Gahbe's hand and saw the diamonds shimmer in his pinky ring. "And gimme that fuckin' ring too nigga." he pulled it off his finger and stared at it. "This shit nice right here, kid. Look at this shit, Ty."

Tyrell grab the ring and examined it. "This shit icy, Six... lemme get this?"

"It's yours kid."

"Good lookin'..." Tyrell put the ring on his pinky finger. "Perfect fit too... yo, hurry up, cars comin' down."

Six stuffed all the money he took into a plastic bag and then cocked his weapon back.

"Easy my nigga, don't do that shit right here." Tyrell grabbed his arm.

Six moved in close on Gahbe and whispered in his ear. “You lucky nigga.” he went to put the gun back on his waistline and had a second thought. “Fuck that.” he gripped the barrel and slammed the butt end of the firearm into Gahbe’s nose and a shot went off.

Gahbe stumbled on the uneven cement; fell against a parked car palming his bloody face and Six ran off into the projects with Tyrell in tow.

CHAPTER NINE

Priscilla was resting on a single bunk staring up at a fly trapped in the light fixture that was mounted to the ceiling. In the back of her mind, she was rooting for that fly to escape its confinement by finding the hole it had once came in through. In a sense, it reminded her of her own struggles and how she was once a prisoner of a certain lifestyle. She thought about what it took to overcome her pain, suffering, and lack of self-confidence. She realized how difficult it was to make that transition and break free from her self-slavery. In spite of all her misfortunes, it felt good to stand on her own two feet and accept responsibility for her doings.

As she gazed, her eyes fell to the bare pale walls, and she reflected on the last couple months of her life. She was fortunate that there was still breath in her lungs, but her heart had been shattered into three pieces and two of those were missing.

After Ms. Kathy located Brandi's whereabouts a few weeks ago, she revealed the news to Priscilla, and ever since then, she's been able to breathe a little bit easier.

Knowing that her daughter was in a safe environment settled Priscilla's nerves, but the fact that she had been in the custody of CPS enraged her.

The very first thoughts to enter her mind were to become rash and extremely violent, but instead, she came to understand that her old ways of handling things would only make the situation more detrimental and further devastate her chances of getting her daughter back.

The process in which she had to endure was a monotonous and tiresome struggle, but it would be the only route to travel at the present time.

In order for Priscilla to regain full custody of Brandi, she needed to show the department of CPS that she's able to keep a paying job, secure adequate living arrangements, and stay alcohol and drug free.

Today Priscilla had the day off from work and wanted to use it to relax and reflect on exactly what she needed to do. Her open custody case with CPS had been going on for two weeks and everything seemed to be in good standing as far as she was concerned. The only dispute she may have had was about having to enter into another drug program after she had recently completed one.

"Priscilla!" Ms. Kathy shouted from the front desk.

She looked at the clock on the wall and then jumped out of the bed. "Yes, Ms. Kathy?"

"Somebody's on the telephone for you… I think it's your job."

My job? It was an hour before she had to be at her drug program. "I hope they ain't asking me to come in today…" she reached for the cordless. "Hello?"

"Hello, Ms. Davis… this is Mr. Porter from Stop & Shop, how are you doing today?"

Priscilla rolled her eyes. "I'm doing pretty good."

She couldn't stand Mr. Porter. He was a black guy trying to be white with no indication of his own heritage and just as ignorant as could be. His horrible breath and the sound of his high pitched voice annoyed most people he came in contact with, so he was definitely a loner.

"Well, that's good Ms. Davis. I'm calling you today because it is very urgent that I speak with you. Is it possible for you to stop by today?"

Speak with me? She was stumped. "Umm... I guess that's not a problem. Can I come in now?"

"Sure; the sooner the better."

"Okay, see you in about twenty minutes." She hung up.

Twenty-two minutes later Priscilla was knocking on Mr. Porter's office door.

"Yes, come in, Ms. Davis." He was wearing his usual, black slacks, black shoes, white collar shirt and a burgundy tie. He pushed some papers aside and sat on the front of his small, steel desk. "Thank you for coming in on such short notice." he reached back and grabbed a folder with some papers in it. "Unfortunately it has been brought to my attention that we may have ourselves a slight problem." he passed Priscilla the folder. "Do you know anything about that?"

When she opened it, the first word she saw was: Grievance

And then she thumbed through the rest of the papers and they were all grievance slips that had her name on them.

"What is this?" she asked, handing the folder back.

"You tell me... I've gotten one of these every week since you've been working here. The reason I took so long to address it is because things have been really busy around here, but it seems like you and Ms. Holland have an issue. Is this correct?" His eyebrows raised and he waited for an answer.

Holland? Priscilla couldn't pin-point the name, but it was definitely familiar. "I'm sorry; I don't know anybody by that name."

Mr. Porter had a hard time believing her. "C'mon, Ms. Davis... *Tara Holland?* The girl who worked at the register you're currently working at."

"Tara!?" She snatched the folder out of Mr. Porter's hand and looked through the papers a second time. "No this bitch didn't..." she mumbled.

"Excuse me?"

"Nothing..." She checked every slip and at the bottom of each one was Tara Holland's John Hancock. "This bitch is lying." Priscilla tossed the folder onto the desk.

Mr. Porter stood up. "Ms. Davis, please... watch your language."

Priscilla was fuming. "Fuck that... that bitch is tellin' a bold face lie. I hope you don't believe any of this Mr. Porter?"

"Well, Ms. Davis you're making it very hard for me not to. What I need to know is... how did you get on that line that you've been working on?"

Priscilla shook her head, she couldn't tell him the truth because that would get Randy in trouble. "Regardless of how I ended up at that register, she's lying on me. I never once threatened that girl's life."

"You know something," He walked to the coffee maker that sat on a table in the left corner of the office and poured a fresh, hot cup. "In matters such as this we usually call the police and let them handle it, but seeing that I've never had a personal problem with you, I opted to just handle it myself—"

Priscilla cut him off before he could finish. "Okay... so what does this mean? What are you gonna do, cut my hours, make me do extra work, what?"

Mr. Porter took a slow sip of his coffee and then peered up at Priscilla. "I'm sorry Ms. Davis, but I'm afraid we're going to have to let you go."

The humming of the air conditioner was the only sound heard for a moment and then Priscilla spoke. "Are you serious?" she smiled and tried to laugh it off. "Let me *go?* I know you're not gonna fire *me* over some lies this little white bitch is makin' up."

"Ms. Davis, you know the final decision is not mines to make. I'm just doing my job."

Priscilla was getting nervous. "Wait..." she sat back down in the chair facing Mr. Porter's desk. "I don't think you understand... I really need this job Mr. Porter. I'm in a difficult situation right now and in order for me to get my daughter back I need to be working. Can you please reconsider?"

Mr. Porter slurped at his coffee. "That's not my concern Ms. Davis, that's your problem. Please slam the door on the way out."

Priscilla lost her temper. "What!?" she jumped in his face and yelled. "Fuck you, you inconsiderate muthafucka!" and she turned to exit.

"Fucking junkie..."

He said it very low and didn't think Priscilla heard him, but as soon as he went to put the cup of coffee to his lips again, a closed, right hand collided with the side of his face and the hot, steamy liquid was everywhere.

Mr. Porter didn't know whether to grab his pounding jaw or his burning chest. "Shit!" he bellowed, stumbling back into the desk.

Priscilla hesitated and then scurried to the door and down the steps.

She could see the exit, but there was so much distance in between, she almost felt like giving up.

The only security guard in the store spotted her out the corner of his eye and figured she was a customer trying to steal something and run out, so he gave chase.

Priscilla dashed through the 'dry foods' aisle and nearly slipped on the fresh, newly waxed floors. When she rounded the corner, one of her arms brushed against some boxes of oatmeal and knocked them to the floor.

"Hey! What the—" A middle aged, Caucasian employee was straightening the shelves and got pushed into them when Priscilla bumped him. He got to his feet and joined the security guard in the foot race.

Everyone's eyes, customers and employees included, were fixed on Priscilla as she frantically raced through the store.

She continued down the long stretch to the exit, turned her head to see how far of a lead she had on her captors and practically ran over an old lady pushing a cart out of the sliding doors. "Excuse me! Sorry!" she yelled back, making it out to the front of the supermarket.

Not knowing which way to go, she had to make a swift decision, but her focus got thrown off when she heard the guard calling out. "Hey you, stop!"

She stepped off the curb and bolted into the street unaware of the black Porsche truck going 20 miles per hour, coming right at her. In order to avoid a deadly collision, the driver had to mash the brake all the way to the floor, and even in doing that, he still hit her.

As soon as he heard the thud on the paneling of the car he threw the vehicle in park and hopped out.

"Oh shit!" He rushed to Priscilla's aid and tried to help her up.

"Ow!" She pulled back when he reached for her arm. "Don't touch me." When she lifted her head, her eyes locked with his and she was frozen for a second; hypnotized by his beautiful, passionate, caring stare.

His skin was the color of almond, his eyes, a slight Hennessy tint and the fragrance he exuded smelled like success. "I'm so sorry. I swear to God, I didn't even see you." He apologized, but noticed Priscilla kept looking back while she was trying to get up. "Is somethin' wrong, you alright?"

"Hey!" The guard screamed out again.

The driver turned and saw the two people running towards them.

Priscilla finally made it to her feet. "Please... can you get me outta here?"

He opened the back driver's side door. "Hurry up, get in."

She dove into the back seat, stretched across the fine leather and her rescuer peeled out of the parking lot.

He stomped on the gas and floored it down Sanford Blvd continuously checking his rearview for anybody trailing. "Where am I going?" he asked, eyes focused on the road. He checked the mirror again and could see that Priscilla was in pain.

"Jus' drop me off in New Rochelle, please..."

The injury was getting the best of her, but she couldn't let it be known.

"Okay, cool..." When he crossed the Pelham borderline, he slowed down in case a patrol car was somewhere in the cut lurking. "What's your name?" he asked.

"Priscilla." She answered.

He came to a stop at a red light at the intersection of Lincoln and Webster Avenue. "Priscilla, my name is Quiane."

"Qui... what?" She wanted to smile, but her arm hurt too badly.

He giggled and pulled off when the light changed. "Quiane," he repeated. "But alotta people call me Q."

"Okay... Owww..." The pain was searing.

"I think you need to get to a hospital. Your arm might be broke."

Priscilla hated being told what to do. "Please, Quiane... Q, whatever... jus' drive."

"No problem." He came to another stop light and asked. "Left or right?"

"Make the right... and you can let me out down the block."

As soon as Quiane pulled to the curb, Priscilla hit the unlock button and rushed out of the truck.

"Hol' up! Wait... where you goin'?" He clicked his seatbelt and hopped out after her. "Priscilla... shit..." she was walking too fast for him.

Without turning around, she yelled. "Thank you, Quiane!" and continued down the block.

He knew he wouldn't be able to catch up to her, so he went back to his truck and cruised down the block when she turned the corner. From where he sat parked, he could see her entering a building, so he waited a few minutes and slowly drove by.

Women's Shelter? He was shocked when he saw the sign on the building.

He made the right, went back around the block, and parked a few car lengths away from the front entrance of the shelter.

For thirty-five minutes Quiane sat parked in his truck, thinking, anticipating, and hoping to get a second chance at seeing Priscilla. She was beautiful and he was uneasy about what had occurred; all he wanted to do was make sure she was alright.

A blue and white patrol car cruised down the block past Quiane's truck and slowed to a stop in front of the shelter. Not even a minute later, an unmarked detective vehicle came up the street from the opposite end and pulled next to the patrol car.

Quiane sat up in his seat and put the key into the ignition when he saw three officers exit the two vehicles.

Ten minutes later, two of the officers came walking out of the building, followed by Priscilla, who was in handcuffs, being escorted by the third officer.

"Shit!" Quiane put the truck in drive and drove off.

CHAPTER TEN

Jasmine fluffed the pillow and placed it back under Mox's head. "Good morning, Mr. Daniels. How are you today?" she went to the window and let the shade up, causing the lambent sunlight to fill the room. "Did you get some rest last night? I heard you were up pretty late."

Mox opened his only good eye and stared at the same picture on the wall that he'd been looking at for the past few days. It had been a week since he snapped out of his coma, but he had yet to utter a word. The only thing he did was put on a half a smile and nod his head; and that only happened once while Jasmine was talking to him.

No one had been by to visit since Priscilla, so the only people to know of his recovery were the doctors and nurses.

Every day for eight, sometimes ten hours, Jasmine would come in to work and tend to Mox's every need. When she first began the job, she had mixed feelings on taking care of someone in a coma. She didn't think she could handle the responsibility of supervising another person's life, but with time came knowledge, and after a few weeks it became second nature.

Jasmine took to Mox even more after she read about his story in the papers. Her heart held regret for all the misfortune he had to withstand and the abrupt transitions he had to encounter. He hadn't said a word to her, but she felt connected to him, almost a part of him, as if they had known each other for most of their lives.

She would arrive at 8:30 am each morning to feed, bathe and massage Mox. Over the past couple of days his skin had begun to regain its color and texture, almost back to its original state.

On a daily basis, Jasmine would read books to Mox, sing for him, play games with him or just sit there and talk to him without him ever expressing the slightest inclination of feeling or speaking a word. He was the perfect listener. He didn't complain, he didn't shout and one of the best parts was, he didn't ask for anything. What Jasmine did notice was that he also never gave up on himself. He fought, every second of every day. It was a struggle, but the work was paying off well.

"Look what I brought in for you today." Jasmine pulled out an iPod Touch from her purse and placed it on the desk beside Mox's bed. "I programmed a few songs in it already, so whenever you wanna listen to some music all you have to do is hit this little, white button right here." she pressed the button and *Amerie's song Why Don't We Fall In Love* was came on. "Ohhh... I love this song!" Jasmine sang the words to Mox.

Why don't we,
Why don't we,
Why don't we faaaall in loooovveeee...

She turned the volume down. "You know how you hear a particular song and it brings you back to the first time you heard it... or it makes you recall that special memory of something or someone... that song right there brings back a lot of memories for me; some of them bad ones, some of them were good." she grabbed the fingernail clipper off the table and began cutting Mox's nails. "It just amazes me how the human brain works."

Mox relaxed and let his head rest on the pillow while the music eased his nerves and rejuvenated his soul. Everything Jasmine did for him, he was appreciative of and as soon as it was possible, he was going to thank her for all that she had done. If it wasn't for her, Mox knew he wouldn't have made it as far as he had. Her caring heart and loving soul was keeping him alive and there was no way he couldn't acknowledge it.

A knock at the door broke Jasmine's concentration. "You can come in Mr. Daniels." She pulled her gloves off and tossed them into the trash. "Oh, I forgot to tell you that you were getting a visitor today Mox."

"Is he awake?" Uncle Earl stepped in slowly, removed his Kangol, and closed the door. He was wearing oatmeal colored, linen pants, chocolate colored suede penny loafers and a V-neck fitted t-shirt to match.

"Yes, he is. He still hasn't spoken a word, but he is slightly responsive and very coherent. He can see you out of his good eye." She grabbed her clipboard and went to exit. "I'll leave you two to talk."

"Hey..." Earl tapped Jasmine's shoulder before she walked out. "What happened to his left eye?"

"When the bullet entered, it permanently damaged his iris and optic nerve in that eye, causing it to remain inoperative. For a while it'll be sensitive to light, so its best that he keep it covered with a patch."

"So you mean to tell me, he's not gonna see out that eye ever again?" he questioned.

"Not likely."

Earl shook his head in disgust. "Damn... does he know?"

"Yes, we've explained everything to him." she replied.

"Fuck!" Earl clenched his Kangol tightly. "Excuse me."

"It's okay." Jasmine opened the door to leave. "If you guys need anything, just press the blue button on the remote that's attached to the bed." She left out.

"Damn, baby boy..." Earl took a deep breath and stared at Mox as he lay in the bed. He wanted to cry, but he had to muzzle his emotions and remain strong for his nephew. He pulled a chair up and sat right next to him. "You lookin' much better nephew. I see you getting' some of your color back too. I know I ain't been around lately, but I got my hands tied up in a few things. Aye, Mox... look at me baby." he stood up so Mox could see how good he was looking. "I done put on about twenty-five pounds, I got money in my pocket, I'm laced up." he grabbed the gold and diamond pendant hanging from the Figaro link around his neck and kissed it. "And best of all... I ain't got high since the day you got shot... and that's the truth Mox. I ain't gon' sit here and lie... shit, it was rough as hell kickin' that shit, but I'm maintainin'. The worst part is over."

Mox focused on the poster hanging on the wall.

"Nephew," Earl scooted his chair in closer to the bed. "I got somethin' big lined up right now..." his voice was low. "I need you wit me baby boy. I need you to get healthy so we can really get this money. It's out here Mox."

"I'm fucked up, Unc..." For the first time, Mox spoke. It was a hoarse mutter, but Earl heard it, smiled and patted Mox on his hand.

"You gon' be alright champ."

"I don't know..." he paused to catch his breath. "If I can fight this shit... Unc..."

Earl sucked his teeth. "Shiiit... aye, Mox... remember when you were little, like five or six years old? You use to beg me every day to teach you how to ride a bike and I kept on tellin' you to wait. Well, I guess you got fed up wit' me sayin' that and you took it upon yourself learn how to ride. First of all, I tried to tell you that the bike you were trying to learn on was too big, but you weren't tryna hear at me at all, so I watched you. I watched you every day for one whole week while you learned to ride that bike. You musta fell about a thousand times, but each time, you got right back up, bruised knees and all, and got back on that bike to try it again." He giggled, paused and then looked in Mox's face.

"That was determination Mox. That was focus. That was you making a vow to self, sayin' that no matter how difficult the task is, you were gonna conquer it. Man... no bullshit... I think you started on a Tuesday and by that weekend you were speedin' all through those projects on that bike. I was proud of you Mox. I couldn't do nothin' but smile when you cam flyin' by me cheesin'. You remember what you said to me?"

Mox didn't speak, he just nodded his head yes.

"You told me you could do anything in the world Mox... you remember that?"

A tear slowly dribbled down Mox's cheek.

"This shit ain't no different..." Earl could no longer hold his emotions captive as the water spilled from his eyes. "You gotta fight Mox... and goddamnit you better not give up on me champ." he wiped the tears from his face with the back of his hand and then checked his Rolex for the time. "Listen man..." he sniffled. "I gotta go take care of a few things, but I'ma come back tomorrow to see you. You want me to bring you somethin'?"

Mox shook his head, no.

"Aight, cool... oh..." Earl reached into his pants pocket, pulled out a picture and tossed it in Mox's lap. "Your aunt is about to move down south and she thought you might like to keep that wit' you. Love you nephew... see you later."

The door shut and Mox's head dropped to the photo sitting in his lap. It was the photo his aunt Sybil had kept on her refrigerator for the past ten years; the photo of his mother.

Mox took a deep breath, exhaled and let the tears spill from his eye.

Excessive torrential rains poured from the heavens, followed by a deep growling thunder, and then a glaring strike of white lightning lit up the sky like fireworks on the fourth day of July.

The projects had been empty all day, devoid of any doings whatsoever; a desert. To make matters worse, two different unmarked detective cars had been rolling through every ten to fifteen minutes.

Tyrell and Six kept dry under their large umbrellas as they stood in front of building 70. “Yo, Ty... who dat?” Six asked, watching a dark grey Town Car pull up to the gate.

Tyrell took a few steps to the middle of the walkway and tried to make out the vehicle. “I don’t know Six, it look like them boys though. You got that on you?”

“Nah, I stashed it in the bushes.”

Tyrell heard the doors come open and walked back to the front of the building. He and Six held their ground and watched the two, six foot white men in dark suits stroll up the strip in their direction.

“Hey, Mikey... what’s the number of that building?” Sammy looked around at the numbers on the two buildings. One had 70 on it and the other had 60.

“Uhh...” Mikey looked at the buildings. “I think it was sixty... yeah, pretty sure it was. We gotta go up to the sixth floor.”

Mikey Telesco and one of his gunmen, Sammy Mallano, trudged through the soaking rain waters and into building 60.

"Who the fuck was that!?" Six skipped up the slanted red wall, dipped into the bushes and came right back out holding a chrome handgun. "Yo, Ty, that wasn't no police."

"Chill... keep that low." Tyrell warned. "Hol' up... lemme call my cousin." He whipped his phone from his pocket and found Dana's number in his contact list, but after three tries he stuffed it back in his pants. "She ain't answering..."

"What door is it, Mikey?" Sammy's Brooklyn accent was deep and rich.

"Six H" Mikey responded as they stepped off the elevator.

Sammy grabbed some black leather gloves out of his pocket and slipped them on his large, rough hands. "So, who is this broad?" He lifted a black, Walther P22 from his waistline and then screwed on the GemTech sound suppressor that he had just bought.

"Her name is Dana... supposed to be one of Mox's broads." Mikey answered.

Sammy cocked the weapon. "Dana, huh?" He put his ear to the door and then backed up. "You know... I been hearin' a lot about this Mox character.... heard he took a bullet in the face... who the fuck he think he is... the Terminator?" Sammy chuckled. "Aye... knock on the door."

Mikey tapped on the door three times.

Sammy cut his eyes at him and shook his head. "You gotta be kiddin' me... Are you serious? Mikey... you got a pair a balls in your pants or a goddamn pussy cat? Knock on the fuckin' door already."

Mikey balled his fist and banged on the door three more times.

"Who is it?" Dana yelled from behind the door.

"It's maintenance!" Sammy smiled and peeked at Mikey.

They could hear her footsteps getting closer and then the sound of a lock being unlatched and then another.

Sammy firmly gripped the weapon with his index finger placed lightly on the hair-trigger, ready to fire.

When the door came open, Dana was standing there with the biggest smile on her face until her eyes dropped down to Sammy's hands. "I thoug—h..."

The shots sounded like three small balloons being popped and then Dana's body just collapsed to the floor.

Sammy tucked the pistol into his inside jacket pocket. "A message from Vinny... don't fuck wit' the Telesco's!" And then he spit on Dana's corpse.

"Them niggas been up there for a minute right, what you think we should do?" Six was anxious.

"Be easy... we jus' gon' play it cool for now, see how this shit play out." The rain started to slow up a bit, so Tyrell let his umbrella down. "Madda fact... I'ma run up the back staircase to see if Dana's upstairs. Stay here, I'll be right back."

When Tyrell made it to the fifth floor, he could hear chatter coming from atop of him on the sixth. He took the steps two at a time and then pulled the stairway door open.

The hallway was packed.

Someone yelled out. "The police said they're on their way!"

Police? Tyrell nudged his way through the speculating tenants.

He saw a trail of blood leaking out of one of the apartments. "Excuse me." his heart sped up and a cold sweat came over him. "I know that ain't..."

He felt a hand on his shoulder trying to turn him around. “Tyrell, c’mere baby… don’t go over there.” the soft voice warned, but it was too late.

The crowd split apart and Tyrell saw Dana, his first cousin, slumped in a river of her own blood at the entrance to her apartment.

He forced his way back through the crowd and ran to the hallway window.

In the midst of the teeming rains, Tyrell could see the two gunmen hurrying out of the building.

He balled his fist and pommeled the thick, glass, window trying to get Six’s attention. “Yo! Yo! Six! Yoooooo!”

Six stood in the rain, oblivious to Tyrell’s cries of vengeance from six flights up as he watched the two suited men get into their car and drive away. By the time he did look up, the hallway was full of people.

The backdoor slammed, Six turned his head and Tyrell came flying down the steps.

“Fuck!’ He screamed loud enough to be heard for miles as he watched the Town Car speed away. He turned to Six with fire flaring in his eyes. “You ain’t hear me fuckin’ bangin’ on the window!?”

Six was stumped. “Nah… I ain’t hear nothin’… what happened?”

He didn’t need an answer once he took a good look at Tyrell’s face.

The tears explained it all.

CHAPTER ELEVEN

Amongst the ramblings, laughter, shifting of chairs, arguments and orange suits, Priscilla could barely remain seated in her chair. Nervous, anxious and afraid of the truth, focused on the Caucasian woman's eyes across from her as the words began to spew from her mouth.

"It's gonna be hard Priscilla. I suggest you take the plea." she said.

"A *plea?* And where does that leave me?"

"Well, first off... they'll lower the charge from a D felony to a B misdemeanor. That alone keeps you from seeing any state time. What happens then is, once you accept the offer, the judge will more than likely sentence you to ninety days jail time."

Priscilla crunched her brows and turned her lip up. "Ninety days?" she shook her head. "I can't do ninety days. I can't do another hour and you're sitting here tellin' me to take ninety days... I have to get my daughter."

The veteran lawyer took a deep breath and tried to be cordial. "Ms. Davis... I don't know how to tell you this, but you getting your daughter back anytime soon is far from a reality anymore. You screwed your chances when you fractured that guys jaw. You're lucky he's not pressing charges."

Priscilla got angry, made a fist and pounded the small table. "Ain't nobody gon' stop me from getting' my daughter back! Not you, not them... nobody!" she shouted. "She's mines!" the tears came down rapidly. "That's my daugh—ter..." she almost couldn't get the words out through her cries.

"Everything alright over here?" A tall, fair skinned C.O. asked.

The lawyer responded. "Yes, everything is good. Sorry sir."

Priscilla buried her face in her arms and sobbed.

"Ms. Davis, there's something else..." The lawyer pulled out a stack of papers that were stapled together and placed them on the table. She tried to explain the situation to Priscilla. "Since you faulted on your attempt to regain custody of Brandi, someone else has stepped in."

Priscilla raised her head immediately. "What? What are you talkin' about, someone else?"

The lawyer ran her finger down the piece of paper, looking for the name. "Oh, a Ms. Anna Mae Davis is now an approved applicant for custody of Brandi. It says here that she's your mother, is this correct?"

Priscilla's heart skipped a beat, dropped to the floor and then broke into tiny pieces and withered away.

"My mother?" She was visibly on the brink of destruction. "I swear to God on every bone in my body if that woman touches a hair on my daughters head... I'ma kill her wit' my bare hands."

"Ms. Davis you need to calm down."

Priscilla stood up out of her seat. "Calm down my ass... bitch you must think I'm stupid. You think I'ma let them take my baby away from me, you're fuckin' wrong!"

Two C.O.s rushed the table and surrounded her. "Have a seat Davis!" one of them advised.

When she ignored the direct order, the taller C.O pulled his cuffs off his waist and his partner grabbed Priscilla by her arms. They forcefully escorted her back to her cell block.

A feeling of discomfort suffused her entire body as she was being dragged off like an animal. "Nooooo! Please don't let them take my baby!" she dissolved in tears. "Please don't let them take her from me!"

3 Days later

"Davis! You got a visit!" The C.O screamed from the bubble.

Priscilla got up from her bunk and walked into the bathroom. She brushed her teeth, washed her face, combed her hair, and changed into some fresh oranges.

The past three and a half weeks she spent at the Valhalla county jail had been a living hell for the first time offender. Despite all the wrong she had done throughout her travels, this had been the only instance where she had been in real trouble. The county jail wasn't too much a far cry from the shelter, but the structure was totally different. There was no option to come and go as you please, and the thought of being told what to do and when to do it didn't sit well with Priscilla.

Her cell was freezing, the food was disgusting and the inmates were filthy, but there was nothing she could do about it at the moment. Priscilla had to bear the brunt, suck it up and make the best of a bad situation.

She walked up to the C.O.'s bubble.

"Don't go down there startin' no shit today, Davis… they were easy on you last time; next one won't be so nice."

He handed her a pass and she waited for an escort to walk her down to the visiting room. When they got there, Priscilla was the only inmate awaiting a search to enter the visiting area, so she got through in a hurry.

"You're at table nine, Davis." The C.O directed.

While she slowly walked towards her table, she could see that her visitor was a female by the way her hair hung past her shoulders.

I hope it ain't this lawyer bitch again. She thought as she got closer.

When she came around the table and saw who it was, she didn't know whether to smile or to cry, so she did both.

"Oh my God, Jennifer!" Priscilla spread her arms and the two friends embraced for the first time in months.

"Girl, you lookin' good..." Jennifer complimented.

They took their seats at the table.

"How did you know I was in here?" Priscilla asked.

"I was here the other day visiting my punk ass baby father and I saw you wild out on that lawyer chick." Jennifer laughed. "What happened, how did you end up in here?"

Priscilla sighed. "Jen... I done
so much bullshit since I left the
crazy. I was stayin' at the shelte
and I even had a job working a
in Mt. Vernon."

"So, what the hell you do to ge

"This lil' bitch at the job was droppin' slips on me, sayin' I was threating her. So on my day off, I get a call from one of the managers and he tells me he needs to talk. I go in there and this self-centered muthafucka fires me, not givin' a fuck about my situation and the fact that I needed the job in order to get my daughter back... so I punched him right in his goddamn nose."

"Wow... so what happened wit' Brandi?"

Priscilla dropped her head. "They got her in the system, Jennifer. I need your help."

Jennifer was stunned. "The system? How— never mind..." she reached over, lifted Priscilla's head and held her hands. "Listen girl... I told you when we was in that program that if you needed *anything* all you had to do was say it. I meant that, Priscilla." she let go of her hands and sat back in the chair. "I don't have many friends, but I do consider you one of the few... and a good one at that. Whatever you need me to do, I got you."

Priscilla smiled and got up to give Jennifer a hug.

"Davis! Sit down!" The C.O. yelled.

"Thank you so much Jennifer." She said, taking her seat.

"No problem girl. How much longer you gotta be in here?"

"I go to court on Monday, that'll make it a full month I been in here. If I accept the plea and get the ninety days, I'll have a month left because you only have to do sixty days out of the ninety."

Jennifer nodded her head. "Okay… so that's not too bad. Well, tell me what you need me to do, so I can get on it."

Priscilla went into detail about what she needed from Jennifer and stressed the importance of how much she appreciated her help.

An hour later she left the visit feeling assured that Jennifer would do the right thing and stay loyal to her word. Her friend's helping hand had assisted Priscilla in easing her mind and focusing on the time that she needed to do. Being stressed out in prison would only lead to more problems.

Sweat continued to fall from Cleo's face as he kept a steady pace while jogging on the treadmill. He looked down at the timer and it read, 7 minutes. "This shit aint no joke Chris. I don't think I can last for three more minutes."

"If you want it, you gotta work hard for it, Cleo. Keep pushing." Chris encouraged.

After Cleo murdered Billy Telesco, he needed a safe haven, so being the good friend; Chris let him crash in his basement until he figured out his next move.

Chris owned a country style, two bedroom, townhouse that was stashed away in the woods somewhere in Rye, New York, a few minutes off the Cross County Parkway. It was hidden in a secluded area, so being spotted was the least of his worries.

Besides that, Cleo had begun to shed some weight due to his excessive cardio training and his overall appearance had taken on a change in the last few weeks. His facial hair had grown, giving him a rough, edgy look and the 30 pounds he dropped had him feeling and looking like a new man.

The treadmill slowed to a stop and Cleo jumped off. "I feel like Tyson in his prime right now." he bounced on his toes and threw a few jabs at the air. "These niggas can't fuck wit' me!"

He looked into the 6 foot wall mirror that leaned against a heavy bag and marveled at himself. He was finally feeling like a leader; doing what he wanted to do whenever he wanted to do it, living life on his terms and his terms only, calling the shots, making decisions; being a boss. But deep within, he feared the truth, the truth of the real him and those unforgotten memories that will forever be embedded in his brain.

As he stood there gazing into the mirror, his mind brought him back to a place that he was reluctant to visit. He thought about the neglect, abandonment and malice of his birth mother and still till this day, Cleo couldn't understand how a person who held a child inside of them for nine whole months could do such a horrible thing.

He closed his eyes and remembered the day Sybil told him the truth about his mother.

"Cleo!... Mox! Stop that goddamn fighting in my house!" Sybil yelled at the two rumbling youngsters.

"He started it!" Cleo squealed as they got up from the floor.

"Stop lying Cleo... you jus' mad because I beat you at your own game."

Cleo was embarrassed. "Shut up!" he sucker punched Mox in the stomach and ran off to the back room.

Sybil saw what happened and darted out of the kitchen to catch him, but the room door slammed before she could get there. "Cleo, open this damn door!" she yelled, turning the knob.

"No!" he screamed back.

She ran back into the kitchen and found a butter knife in the drawer. "You must think I'm playin' wit' you boy." She fidgeted at the lock with the knife, trying to get the door open. Seconds later, she got it.

"What I tell you about puttin' your hands on your cousin?" Sybil scolded.

Cleo sat at the edge of the bottom bunk, crying and holding onto an envelope.

"What the hell you cryin' for, what is that?" She snatched the envelope from his hands and when she saw what it was, her bottom lip dropped. "Oh God, Cleo did you read this?"

He didn't answer; he just wiped the tears and looked up at her with a face full of anguish.

"I'm sorry, Cleo..." Sybil sat next to him on the bed. "Listen, your mother's not a bad person, she just happened to make some not so good choices in life."

Cleo's voice was low. "So, it is true?"

Sybil took a deep breath and tried to figure out how to tell Cleo the truth. "Listen Cleo... your mother and I were best of friends back when we were in high school. We did everything together and when I say everything, I mean... everything. Your mother was gorgeous. She just had that look; tall, petite and extremely beautiful. All she ever wanted to do was be a runway model. That's all she ever talked about. Day in and day out, every conversation had something to do with modeling. She dreamed of making it big and moving to Paris somewhere. We joked a lot, but that was one thing that she was truly passionate about."

Sybil gathered herself when she felt her emotions starting to build. She pulled a tissue from her pocket and patted the tear on her cheek.

"When we were in high school, there was this guy named Michael Brown who was the star of the varsity basketball team at the time. Well, all the girls in the school were dying to get a piece of Mr. Brown, but Michael had the biggest crush on your mother. He would've gone to the end of the earth for her if need be. Whatever she asked for, she got, but the only problem was; your grandfather was not having it. He could never accept the fact that the Brown family was from the projects. He hated the Brown family... for what reasons, I don't know, but what I do know is that your mother and Michael secretly got together and a few months later, she ended up pregnant. Boy was your grandfather pissed."

Cleo sat quietly, listening to Sybil. He was trying to absorb every word she was saying.

"At first, he tried to make her get an abortion, but she wouldn't do it and he couldn't force her to, so he acted as if everything was okay. Then he played on your mother's dream of becoming a model and made her believe that having a child would destroy her body and she would never get the chance to walk the runway. She believed him, and two days after she gave birth to you, I got a knock on my door.

"Girl, what the hell you doin' out the hospital?" Sybil brushed the crust from her eyes and stepped aside to let her best friend enter the apartment.

Vivian's hands shook as she rushed through the door, holding her newborn son wrapped in a blanket. "Sybil, I need the biggest favor in the world." she put the baby down on the couch and sat on the wooden coffee table.

"And what's that?" Sybil reached down and picked the newborn up.

"I need you look after my son."

She rocked the baby in her arms. "Look after him... where you goin?"

Vivian got up and paced the living room floor. "Sybil I got a dream." She said, reaching into her purse for a cigarette. "Right now, I don't have time for no cryin' baby."

"Cryin' baby?" Sybil was shocked. "Vivian, this is your child. You carried this child for nine months and now you just gon' give 'em away?"

"No... I'll be back, I promise." She lied. "I jus' need some time Sybil. A little bit of time to sort this out and do what I need to do. I can't be a world famous model if every ten minutes, I have to worry about this baby."

Sybil looked down at the baby in her arms. He was sound asleep, unknowing of the world in which he had been brought into. "I can't take care of no baby, Vivian. I got my own responsibilities."

Vivian put the cigarette out in the ashtray. "Please, Sybil... jus' for a few months, and as soon as I get myself in order, I swear to God I'll be back for him." she quickly walked to the door and opened it. "You got my word on that."

Sybil tried to put the baby down and catch her before she walked out. "Wait... Vivian... I can't..." The front door slammed and Sybil was left standing there holding a three day old baby boy. She shook her head, sighed and looked at the precious human life in her arms. "I don't know the first thing about takin' care of no baby." she voiced aloud. "At least she could've told me your name..."

Sybil held the envelope in her hand and looked over to Cleo. "And that's how you ended up here. Nobody asked questions or anything. You were jus' a new addition to the family, and it's always been that way. When the people close to me asked where the baby came from, I always told them that you were adopted."

"Who gave me my name?" He asked.

"My brother Earl came up with that name for you. He helped me out a lot in the beginning and that's why we're so close now." Sybil ripped a piece of paper out of a notebook and wrote something on it. "Here, this is your mother's real name, last address and phone number. Maybe one day you could write to her." she passed Cleo the paper.

He stared at it and asked. "What does she look like?"

"Hold on..." she went into the other room and came right back holding a picture.

When Cleo saw the picture he couldn't believe his eyes. His mother was beautiful. She was tall, brown skinned with big lovely brown eyes and a physique that you only saw in magazines.

"She's pretty ain't she?"

Cleo nodded yes.

"Cleo," Sybil sat back on the bed next to him. "we need to keep this between us. Can this be our little secret?"

He nodded yes again, but in his heart, he didn't agree and he knew one day that the truth would come out.

Cleo snapped out of his daze and went over to the corner of the basement to his bag, and pulled out his wallet. He thumbed through some papers and found what he was looking for.

"Wanna take a road trip Chris?" He asked, looking down at the small piece of paper with a name, number and address on it.

"Where we going?"

Cleo just smiled and said. "South..."

CHAPTER TWELVE

Frank's establishment, Club RED, was located somewhere between West 16th St. and 10th Avenue in lower Manhattan. Prior to it becoming a night club, the space housed a wholesale market that, after a few years, eventually went out of business.

After obtaining a bachelor's degree in business management, Frank decided to put his education to use and legitimize a significant portion of his illegal drug money. He renovated the space and had a night club built.

Club RED had two floors, two large half circle bars, six 40 inch flat screen televisions and the color red everywhere.

The spot was filled to capacity as Frank and Nate, both fitted in three thousand dollar designer suits, relaxed on the ritzy suede V.I.P couches in a cordoned off area at the rear of the club. A champagne bucket filled with ice, two bottles of Ace of Spade Brut Rose, and a few drinking glasses sat on the table in front of them, not to mention, they were surrounded by a bevy of beautiful women.

Frank tapped Nate on his shoulder and leaned in close to his ear to say something. "Did you tell him to be here on time?" he glanced at the rose gold Rolex on his wrist.

Nate nodded yes and then sipped his bubbly.

"Well where the fuck is he?"

A few minutes later, a six foot, 300 pound, black, gorilla looking security guard made his way over to where Frank and Nate sat. "There's a gentleman out here accompanied by two others saying that they're here to see you, boss."

"Let him in." Frank replied.

When the bouncer came back, Tyrell, Six and Uncle Wise were following him.

"Gentlemen, have a seat." Frank greeted the men and offered them drinks.

"So, wassup?" he looked at Tyrell.

"Man... I done looked all over for that nigga Cleo, and one thing I do know is... he ain't in New York."

Frank didn't believe that. "What the fuck you mean he ain't in *New York?* Where can he go?"

"I don't know, but he ain't out here. I had my people check every borough, every nook and every muthafuckin' cranny... he ain't out here Frank, I'm tellin' you."

The disappointment was obvious. "You told me you was gon' handle this." Frank stood and faced Tyrell.

"I am."

"When?"

Tyrell caught the eye of a seductive, redbone goddess with short blonde hair walking by, and winked at her. Then he said, "Don't worry Frank... I got this. In the meantime, let's toast."

"To what?"

Tyrell raised his glass. "To the power of the muthafuckin' dollar!" he shouted and they all did the same. He stepped in a little closer to Frank. "I'm pretty sure you know Uncle Wise, but this is my partner, Six." he said.

"Hey Frank," Uncle Wise downed another cup of bubbles. "I went by to see Mox the other day... y'all been by there?"

Lately Frank had been feeling guilty about not going to visit Mox on a regular basis, but he attributed it to working long hours, running the club, and maintaining his drug business. He knew it was a worthless excuse, but that was the only way he could bring himself to justify his actions. Mox was like a brother to him and now he felt like he should've made a better effort to be there for him.

"I can't do, it Unc. I ain't even gon' lie. I know I been fuckin' up by not being by his side, but I can't see my boy like that; that shit hurts too much."

"How is he?" Nate jumped in.

Uncle Wise poured another drink. "He's doin' much better. I spoke to him on the phone today and he said they were gonna move him to a rehabilitation center in Greenwich Connecticut."

Frank and Nate replied at the same time. *"Connecticut?"*

"That's what *I* said... I guess that's what it is though. I think they moving him on Monday."

"Hey Frank, I think we should take a ride up to CT and check on him." Nate suggested, but was ignored.

Frank refilled everybody's glass with champagne and then summoned the waitress over and ordered her to bring two more bottles.

Tyrell sat down next to Frank on the couch. "I need a favor Frank… actually, two."

"I'm listening."

"What you know about this dude?" He slid Frank a piece of a napkin with a name written on it.

Frank leaned over and showed Nate the name. "What he got to do with anything?" he asked.

"He had my cousin Dana killed." Tyrell answered.

"*Dana?* Get the fuck outta here… when did this happen?"

"'Bout a week ago… they're havin' her funeral tomorrow."

Frank thought about the situation and realized the Italians weren't going to let up, *but Dana?* That was something he would have never expected. "Damn… I'm sorry to hear that, but you think you ready for that?"

"*Ready?* Shit..." Tyrell glanced at Six. "I came into this world ready."

"You know it's sharks in that water kid. Don't jump in if you can't swim, you might drown."

Tyrell let the words sink in and thought about what Frank was trying to tell him. He was just a child, a teenager, trapped in a world of sin that was ruled by grown men, where every choice he made had to be decisive, quick witted and vigorous. He knew he was short the manpower to wage a war against the Telesco's, but his emotions were blinding his perception of reality. "They killed my cousin, Frank..." he took a sip of his champagne and then wiped his lip with the back of his hand. "I'ma murder every one of them muthafuckas..."

Blonde hair walked by again, but this time she stopped, bent down and whispered something in Tyrell's ear.

He smiled and said, "Yeah, jus gimme a minute." When she stepped off he turned to Frank. "Who the fuck is *that* bitch?"

Frank shrugged his shoulders. "I seen her around a few times, don't know her though. What's this other favor you talkin' about?"

"I been gettin' my feet wet in the game a lil' somethin'... and uhh, I got my team." He looked back at Earl and Six. "Uncle Earl's tryna guide me in the right direction, but I need some more help. I figured that's where you could come in."

Frank was confused. "I don't get it."

"Listen," Tyrell lowered his voice just enough so that Frank could hear him. "Word is, you the king of coke."

Frank smiled and then he shook his head. "Do you realize what you jus' sat here and told me? You want me to supply you, and you being guided in the right direction by a fuckin' *dope fiend?"*

Uncle Earl heard every word. "Aye, Frank you better watch your mouth."

"No disrespect Unc, don't take it the wrong way."

Earl was fuming. He hadn't felt this way in years. It was like he was living his second childhood and he was ready to take it back to the old school one more time just to show these so called gangsters how shit is done. He was itching for Frank to say something else slick, Mox's homeboy or not, he was about get it. He was about to bring the old Wise Earl out of retirement.

"Take it the wrong way my ass, *you* said it muthafucka. You better curb that tongue before I remove it."

"Fellas, easy... easy..." Nate squeezed between the two men. "Let's not even go there wit' it tonight. It's a bunch of beautiful women in here, we got champagne, good music... lets jus' relax and enjoy ourselves... please."

The men separated and continued to enjoy their night out.

Tyrell bumped Frank on the shoulder. “So, I guess that means no?”

Greenwich Woods Rehabilitation Center
1 Week later

After continuous progress while in the hospital, Mox was moved to a rehab center in Greenwich, Connecticut to further his development. The 217 bed facility is set on elegantly landscaped private and secured grounds, and has a wide variety of staff to cover all aspects of the rehabilitation process.

Mox was staying in room 403 which was located on the far west end of the building. His window overlooked a giant lake and hundreds of miles of nature's greenery.

He sat quietly in his wheelchair facing the window, rubbing his beard, staring out at the sunshine of the midday, and trying to figure out a way to get back home. He took a deep breath and inhaled the aroma of the fresh fall season.

A tap on the door caused him to turn around and see who was entering his room.

It was one of his doctors. "Mr. Daniels, how are you doing today?" he inquired, closing the door after entering.

"Not too good, doc." Mox was talking regular again, but he was still physically weakened. He barely had enough strength to cross his legs. "How come I can't remember certain things, doc?"

"Things like what?"

"You know, small shit like... my favorite color or favorite food. Shit... sometimes I can't even remember what happened."

The doctor pulled a pen from the front pocket on his shirt and jotted down a few words on his clipboard. "I see... What about your name, birthday... things like that?"

"I remember those."

"Umm hmm..." The doctor flipped the pages on the clipboard and sat in the chair alongside the wall. "Well, Mr. Daniels... I believe you may be suffering from a slight case of either amnesia or dementia."

"Amnesia?"

"Yes, nothing severe, but it will take some re-learning of some of your basic motor skills. Do you have any family members that can bring in old pictures or something?"

Mox looked out at the marvelous landscape. "Nah... no family, it's jus' me."

"Okay, that's not a problem, sir... tomorrow morning we can get started on your therapy. It's all up to you Mr. Daniels, if you make the effort, the work will eventually pay off." The doctor closed the clipboard and left the room.

Mox rolled himself over to the front of the dresser and gazed at his reflection in the mirror. He placed his left hand over the patch on his eye, took a deep breath and a tear came rolling down the right side of his cheek.

The battles had taken a toll on his physical abilities and he felt beneath himself. He felt useless and forgotten, worn out and battered. He couldn't understand how he had been able to take another breath and more than often, he thought about why God chose to keep him here and remove everyone else from his life.

The telephone rang and it startled Mox for a second. He wondered who could be calling if no one knew where he was at, but then he thought about Uncle Wise and went to pick it up. "Hello?"

The voice on the other end was deep and groggy. "You know this ain't over until every one of you monkeys is in a grave." And he hung up.

Mox knew exactly who it was.

He squeezed the cordless phone tightly in his hands and then tossed it into the mirror, causing shattered glass to cover the top of the dresser.

If the Italians knew where he was, then it was only a matter of time before they showed up for a visit; that is, if they weren't already in the building.

CHAPTER THIRTEEN

Priscilla stepped out of the county jail gates, looked up to the cloudless azure sky and thanked God for giving her yet another opportunity to do the right thing. The positive attitude she adapted from being in the program and staying at the shelter had been lost the second that police officer put those cuffs on her wrist.

The passive, cordial and respective Priscilla wasn't getting the job done. It was time to make a change.

"You better smile girl, you outta there now." Jennifer greeted her friend with a big hug and handed her a brown paper bag.

Priscilla ripped the bag open and started counting the bills.

"It's all there, don't even trip… but that sweat suit…" Jennifer frowned.

"I know, I know, don't even start."

"Girl… hurry up and get in this car so we can go shoppin'."

Priscilla opened the passenger side door to the 2009 gun metal Nissan 350z. "This is a nice car Jennifer. Let me find out you gettin' some paper out here..."

"I damn sure ain't gon' be out here starvin'" she replied.

The two women got into the vehicle and took off for the highway.

"Did you get the info I asked for?" Priscilla questioned, snapping her seatbelt in.

"Yup," Jennifer dipped through the traffic, hit the blinker and turned onto the Sprain Brook parkway. "Now listen... I went through hell gettin' this info, but it was for a good cause, so I'm not complainin'. Okay, first... Mox is doing much better, they say he's talkin' and movin' around."

Priscilla's face was beaming with pleasure when she heard Jennifer mention Mox's recovery.

"The only thing is... they moved him to some rehabilitation center up in Greenwich Connecticut."

"*Greenwich?* Why would they send him there?"

"I have no idea, but the address is in the glove compartment."

"What about Brandi?" Priscilla was anxious.

"Okay... the good news is, your mother wasn't able to get custody of her, but she has been placed with a family."

"Dammit!" Priscilla's voice went high. "Oh my God... I can't imagine what my baby is goin' through." Her eyes started to water up. "How am I gonna get her back now? Lord... please... help me."

Jennifer touched Priscilla's shoulder. "Don't worry about it girl, everything gon' be alright. I got a plan. I know exactly where she is, and we can get her back, but we have to move fast."

"Jennifer, please... I'll do anything to get my baby back in my arms..." A tear drop rolled down the side of her face. "Anything..."

After a few hours of shopping in the Westchester Mall, Priscilla and Jennifer made their way downstairs to the Cheesecake Factory to sit, eat and discuss the details of the plan.

"Dang girl, slow down... that food ain't goin' nowhere."

Priscilla looked up with a mouth full of food. "You ever eat a Valhalla food tray?"

"Hell no..."

"Well, me either." She wiped her mouth with the napkin in her lap. "The whole time I was there, I didn't touch those nasty ass trays... all I ate was honey buns, soups and pre-cooked rice."

"I see..." Jennifer laughed. "You put on a few pounds too."

Priscilla rolled her eyes. "Please, don't remind me." She took a sip of the virgin daiquiri in front of her. "So; what's this plan you talkin' about?"

A waiter came by to collect their empty plates and refill their drinks.

"Okay... look, I found the family that Brandi is stayin' with. It's some white lady and her husband down in Harrison, she—"

"Is she alright?" Priscilla was apprehensive.

"Yes, she's fine. They got money so she's well taken care of... trust me."

Priscilla was still worried. "Are you sure? How do you know?"

Jennifer reached into her Dooney & Bourke handbag and grabbed her I-phone. "Here... look."

It was a picture of Brandi, in a park, playing on the swings.

Priscilla stared at the phone. "This is all my fault." she said, feeling guilty. "If I would'a done better, she wouldn't be in this situation. I can't blame nobody but myself." she sniffled and the agony of separation got the best of her, causing her to break down and cry, like a child who couldn't get what they desired.

Jennifer rubbed her shoulder. "Stop beatin' yourself up, Priscilla. I told you, I got a plan... we can get her back."

Immediately, she looked up. "How?"

Jennifer dabbed at the corners of her mouth with a napkin and sipped her water. "Every Saturday afternoon they bring Brandi to the park for an hour to let her run around. The same park, the same hour… every weekend, and each time it's the same routine. I got it mapped out... look, all we gotta do is be there when they are, and as soon as she takes her eyes off her… we snatch her! What you think?"

As bad as Priscilla wanted to buss out laughing, she didn't. The situation was too serious, but she couldn't help but to find a bit of humor in the matter.

"That's it? That's your plan?"

Jennifer attempted to keep a straight face, but Priscilla's smirk made it impossible.

"I'm sayin'… it's a start."

They laughed together.

"A *start?"* Priscilla said. "You had a whole month to think about what the plan was and this is what you came up *with?"*

Jennifer tried to convince her. "I'm tellin' you… I know it can work."

"I guess it's gonna have to work." she replied, finishing her drink. "It's the only thing I got right now... so, what about the other thing?"

"Oh, he said he wants to meet wit' you tomorrow afternoon, in the city."

The next morning, Priscilla rose out of bed as the fulgent sun ascended into the crisp luminous sky. A cool autumn breeze brushed by her face and the flute like chirping of a House Sparrow sitting on the sill reminded her of how fortunate she was.

Her feet touched the lush two thousand dollar carpet and she got down on her knees, clasped her hands together and bowed her head in prayer.

"God grant me the serenity to accept the things I cannot change; courage to change the things I can; and wisdom to know the difference. Amen."

The door opened shortly after she finished and Jennifer sashayed into the room wearing just panties and a bra, holding a tray with a plate of food and a glass of orange juice.

Her body was amazing. She had a permanent tanned complexion that gave her a glow, long, dirty blonde hair, a nice handful of breasts and an ass like a Brazilian porn star.

"Good mornin', sleeping beauty." she giggled. "I wanted you to awake to a surprise, but you're already up, so... here you go." she passed the tray to Priscilla and then pulled the curtain on the window open to let more light in.

Priscilla sat at the edge of the Queen sized bed with the tray on her lap, staring down at the food, trying to figure out how Jennifer knew everything she liked.

Turkey bacon.

French toast.

One fried egg, a bowl of diced fruit and fresh squeezed orange juice.

"Are you a physic or somethin'?" she joked, picking the fork up.

"Why you say that?"

"Because, everything on this plate is my favorite."

"Really? This is my breakfast every morning." Jennifer picked the remote up, pushed power and the 50 inch flat screen television mounted to the wall lit up.

Priscilla finished off the bowl of fruit. "Not to be in your business or anything, but how the hell can you afford a place like this?"

Jennifer owned a one bedroom, townhouse style condo on North Main St. in East Hampton, Connecticut. The seven hundred square foot home had cathedral ceilings, a loft bedroom, jetted tub and a separate shower enclosure. At the time she bought it, Jennifer paid $110,000 cash, but with the renovations, it's now worth well over $150,000.

She smiled at herself in the giant mirror attached to the sandalwood dresser. "Do it the right way..." she seductively licked her lips and then winked her eye when she saw Priscilla was watching. "And you can get anything you desire from a man."

"Ill, nasty."

"Shut up." Jennifer tossed a scarf at Priscilla. "Don't act like you ain't never did somethin' strange for some change."

"Huh... haven't we all."

For Priscilla, it felt good to be able to laugh and enjoy the moment, because for the past few months she had been seeing more gloomy days than bright ones. The effects of her burdens were weighing heavy on her mentally. It was impossible to push aside her problems and act as if nothing was wrong, so she took responsibility for her actions and decided the only way things would change, is if she had a hand in changing them.

She got up to bring the dishes back into the kitchen, but didn't get out the door.

"Oh shit, Priscilla...look!" Jennifer turned the volume up on the television.

Haitian authorities say they seized six hundred and sixty pounds of cocaine from a hidden compartment on a private boat about fifty miles west of the capital city this morning. The three hundred kilograms have a wholesale value of three million dollars and a street value of over ten million. The seizure comes amid increasing pressure to bring an end to the drug smuggling in Haiti, which United States government believes is a main shipping point for Columbian cocaine bound to the states.

"Wow." Jennifer's eyes were glued to the television. "I wouldn't even know what to do wit' all them drugs."

Priscilla thought different; she knew exactly what she would do with them and she also understood the ins and outs of the coke game. "Somebody's gonna be *really* pissed today."

"I bet they are." Jennifer hit power and went to her closet to find some clothes to throw on. "Forget that, we got a nine o clock appointment at the hair dresser and your meeting is at two."

"Hair dresser?"

"Yup, I'ma have my girl, Vee, at the shop hook you up. Watch... you gon' love it."

Two hours later, Priscilla stood in front of the full body mirror at the back of the beauty salon in a stupefied gaze, trying to figure out who was the person staring back at her. "Oh-my-God... look at my hair." she reached back and felt the long, silky weave that was sewn into her roots.

Jennifer was probably the most excited. "I told you she was the best! Oohh, you hooked her up!" she examined Priscilla's new hair. "This is really nice. I might have to get mine done like this." She laughed. "How much do I owe you Vee?"

"Eight hundred."

Jennifer peeled off ten one hundred dollar bills and handed them to Vee. "Enjoy the rest of your week Vee. I'll be in next week so you can trim my edges."

When they got back into the car, Priscilla was still in shock. "Eight hundred dollars, Jennifer? Damn..."

"It's a lil' pricey, but it's worth it. That Indian hair is the best you can get. Don't worry about it... that was my gift to you; now we gotta hurry up. You only got an hour before your meeting."

Priscilla was so wrapped up in the way her hair looked, that the meeting had slipped her mind. "Oh shoot, the meeting... what am I gonna wear?"

"That's hot on you!" Jennifer complimented as Priscilla fixed the straps on her rose petal colored, convertible Jersey gown.

"One strap or two?" she asked.

"I think you should go wit' the two." Jennifer answered. "I'll meet you downstairs in the car."

Priscilla gazed at her reflection in the mirror and thought about how far she had come. All the drudgery she had put herself through prepared her for what she was about to encounter. It was like the turning of a page to a new chapter in her life; a clean slate; a fresh start; a brand new beginning.

She fixed the straps on her shoulder and went downstairs to meet Jennifer in the car.

On the drive to Manhattan, Priscilla was antsy and impatient, but truly excited about attending her meet. If everything went as expected, she could end up in a prominent position; a space that she hadn't been accustomed to in a long time.

Jennifer slowed up and pulled to the curb at 190 Sullivan Street. "This is the place." she said, reaching into her purse. She handed Priscilla a cell phone. "If you need anything, just call me. My number is already programmed."

Priscilla got out the car and walked past the four tables outside and entered the restaurant.

A short, overweight Spanish guy behind the bar greeted her. "Hola, senora. Welcome to Salon de Tapas."

A small, candle lit diner located in a well-trodden section of Manhattan, Salon de Tapas is beloved for its prompt service, wide variety of tapas and reasonable pricing.

The six small tables with burning candles, along the brick wall were all vacant.

Priscilla took a seat at the last table, about fifteen feet away from the kitchen, and she waited. After thirty-five minutes, she made up her mind to leave. She got up and started to call Jennifer.

"You leaving already?"

Before she took her eyes off the phone, she recognized the voice. It was one she could never forget. That familiar scent she knew all too well, tickled her nose and made her smile inside.

"It's been a long time Juan Carlos." She took a step forward and reached out to shake his hand.

His appearance hadn't changed much at all. He was still the tall pretty boy with the curly black hair, gold Cuban link chain, and chipped tooth.

"You look beautiful." He said, removing his $4,000 Brioni dinner jacket.

When he took his seat, he picked up the menu, and the glare from the light above hit one of the flawless diamonds in his pinky ring.

"I see you still livin' a lucrative lifestyle."

"Everything you see is not always what it appears to be." he replied.

"Here you go wit' your philosophies."

Juan Carlos looked over the menu while he continued to talk. "You know how this business is, Priscilla. You get respect when you attain a certain level of success, and even then, that respect is short lived. Those who once respected you now become jealous and envious of you, and depending on the situation... they may even have bad blood towards you. There's always somebody that wants your spot, so don't ever forget that." he looked up into Priscilla's eyes. "Aint no time to get complacent in this business... it's all about your next move."

The waiter approached their table. "Are you ready to order, sir?"

"I'll just have a seltzer water with some fresh lime please, and the television remote control. Priscilla, are you hungry?"

"No, I'm fine. I do need your help though."

He smiled. "That's funny. I need your help too."

Not long after, the waiter returned and placed the glass of seltzer water and a plate with fresh, sliced lime next to Juan Carlos. "Here's the remote, sir."

"I already know what you need," he said to Priscilla. "I've been in this game long enough. I can see it in your eyes, but in order for you to get what you want, I'm going to need you to take care of something for me." he dug into his inside pocket and pulled out a picture.

"Who is she?" Priscilla looked at the salt and pepper haired woman.

"La Capitana... she's in charge of the second biggest cocaine distribution ring in the U.S., and by far, the most ruthless bitch on the face of this earth. She was once a business partner of mine, but the stipulations of our venture weren't to her liking, so she decided to play for the other team." Juan Carlos hit a button on the remote, and the television that was mounted to the wall on the other side of the diner came on. He flicked through the channels until he found what he was looking for. "Have you seen this?"

It was the same breaking news story she had watched at Jennifer's house.

"I saw it this mornin'"

"Three hundred birds, Priscilla." He shook his head and then rubbed his face with his hand. "There's no way I can let this go uncontested."

"And where do I come in?"

"I need someone outside of my people for this."

"And so you choose me?"

"I wouldn't ask if I didn't think you were capable of getting it done... besides, Mox owes me." Juan Carlos grinned and winked his eye at Priscilla. "You want something. I want something... if we work together, I'm pretty sure we can come to an agreement that would benefit all parties involved."

Priscilla was in awe of his proposition. "You askin' me to take somebody's life, Juan Carlos. I don't know if I'm ready for that..."

"When a general sends his troops into battle do you think for one second he's not aware of the capabilities of his soldiers?" he picked a lime up and squeezed the juice into his water. "He's absolutely cognizant of their abilities, Priscilla. This is why he is the general... It's all about catching your enemy off guard. No matter how well thought out the plan is, you can never account for the element of surprise."

"Yeah, but what if it doesn't go right... then what?"

I would never lead you into something that I thought you weren't qualified for, Priscilla. It's only as difficult as you make it. I got everything set up. All you have to do is show up and execute the plan."

"Show up and execute the plan, huh?" Priscilla sat back and a look of hostility came over her face.

She knew there was no other option. She had gone every route she could possibly go and time was something that was not on her side. A decision had to be made, and it had to be made quickly.

Juan Carlos looked at Priscilla and raised his eyebrow. He didn't even wait for her answer. He just got up, wrote a phone number on a napkin and walked out of the diner.

CHAPTER FOURTEEN

A light drizzle fell from the dark colored sky as the churchgoers filed out of the chapel. All the smiling faces were an indication of the good word from Rev. Miguel Diaz, who was the congregation's senior pastor for the last ten years at the Bronx Spanish Evangelical Church.

"Would you like me to sit and wait, La Capitana?"

"No, I'll be just fine. Wait for me in the car." She answered.

The brawny, slick haired bodyguard did as he was told and went to wait in the car.

Priscilla, unseen, wearing a black suit skirt, black shoes, and matching gloves, stood across the street watching the church empty out. If a move was going to be made, the time couldn't have been any better.

Her eyes were focused on the target as she remembered the details that Juan Carlos explained to her.

La Capitana never leaves the house without armed guards, so the only way to get close to her would be on a Sunday afternoon, at church while she's making her confession.

The thought of taking someone's life while they confessed their sins didn't sit right with Priscilla, but it was too late. The call had been made, and the clock was about to expire. In the back of her mind, she knew that if she didn't go through with this, Juan Carlos would have *her* killed. It would have nothing to do with their personal relationship; everything thrived off business.

Slowly, she crept across the dampened street when she saw the target going back into the church. Pellets of rain splashed her face as she moved closer and closer to the entrance, her thoughts racing through her brain like the 450 Motocross.

La Capitana turned the knob on the confession room door, sat down on the small wooden stool, and faced the grated window to confess her sins.

She made the sign of a cross with her hand and bowed her head. "In the name of the Father, and of the Son, and of the Holy spirit; my last confession was one month ago. I sit before you to confess my sins of murder, adultery and dishonor. I am sorry for these and all the sins of my past life. Lord Jesus, son of God; have mercy on me, a poor sinner."

The priest spoke. "Give thanks to the Lord, for he is good."

They made the sign of a cross together and then she said. "For his mercy endures forever... Amen."

The Priest got up and left, but when La Capitana reached for the door knob, it was already coming open.

Priscilla slithered through the small, cracked door like a cheetah in the jungle after nightfall when hunting its prey. Knife in hand; their eyes locked and she whispered. "You scared?"

The lump in La Capitana's throat stalled her words, but they eventually came out. Her voice was soft, but firm, and her focus was directly on Priscilla. "You should be asking yourself that question. Hurry up and do your job."

Fear was an emotion that had been left out of La Capitana's life as a child. The only thing she had ever been afraid of was dying poor and being buried in a cardboard box.

Priscilla hesitated, and then she lunged at her target.

The 5 ½ inch parkerized blade sunk into La Capitana's soft flesh.

As Priscilla shoved the knife inside of her, she felt the blade hit a bone. She grabbed the back of her neck and pushed harder, causing the stainless steel dagger to go deeper into her abdomen.

A spill of blood crawled out the side of La Capitana's mouth and her body relaxed.

Minus the faint beating of Priscilla's heart and the sporadic short breaths that La Capitana held onto, the room was silent.

Priscilla let her body crumple to the hard wood floor, stepped over her and exited the church unnoticed.

"You have to eat something, Mox, c'mon... it's been two and a half days." Jasmine tried to convince Mox to touch the plate of food in front of him.

"I aint hungry."

"At least try one of my cookies. I stayed up all night baking these for you."

"I didn't ask you to do that, so don't sit here and try to make me feel guilty about it."

Jasmine was open-mouthed. She had never heard Mox speak in such a fashion. "Sorry for caring... sheesh."

It was the second day in a row that Jasmine had come to visit Mox at the rehabilitation center and it was the second day in a row she had been thrown shade.

"Jus' leave me alone right now, Jasmine. I don't feel like being bothered."

"Is *that* what I'm doing Mox?" Jasmine was outraged. "Bothering you? I've done nothing but help you from the day I walked into that hospital room, and now that you're getting a little better you're feeling yourself. Fuck you Mox!" Jasmine snatched her purse and jacket off a hanger in the closet and stormed out the room.

"Jasmine… wai—"

The door slammed, and once again, Mox was left alone; solo, just him, and his curious thoughts. The exact same thoughts that continued to strain his mental and demolish his self-confidence.

Mox's recovery hadn't been advancing as rapidly as he'd expected, and he still hadn't gained the strength to stand on his own two feet. The determination was still present, yet his faith was becoming slighter and more displaced.

He rolled himself over to the dresser, stuffed his earphones into his ear, and pressed play on his iPodTouch.

The elevator door was closing and Jasmine nearly ran into Priscilla and Jennifer trying to catch it before it went back down. "Excuse me, sorry." She apologized, brushing by the two women.

Priscilla recalled the face, but couldn't figure out where she had seen her before. "I know her from somewhere..." she mumbled.

They continued down the long corridor stretch and stopped in front of room 209 and Jennifer said, "I think this is the room."

But Priscilla's mind was someplace else. "I knew I recognized that girl's face. That's the chick from the hospital..."

"Huh, who?" Jennifer had no clue as to what Priscilla was rambling about.

"The bitch that jus' got on the elevator. She was at the hospital when Mox was there."

"At the hospital, so what is she doin' here?"

"I don't know, but I'm damn sure gon' find out." She turned the knob and pushed the door open.

Mox had his back turned when Priscilla and Jennifer walked in and didn't realize they were present until he heard the door close.

"Who is that?" He said, turning in his wheelchair.

Priscilla stiffened at the sight of his uncovered eye, a chill shot through her body and the hairs on her arm stood up. For a moment, she was scared, but there was no denying the fact that her love for the man sitting less than ten feet away from her was continuously burning like a wild brush fire.

Before a word was said, an avalanche of tears slid down her face, smudging what little bit of make-up she had on.

"I miss you Mox..." she bent down to give him a hug and he wrapped his arms around her.

"Please... get me outta here." he begged.

Jennifer watched as the two embrace and shared a long awaited moment. She had finally got to see the man she had heard so much about, and even with one eye, he was still as handsome as ever.

Priscilla wiped her face dry and began searching the room for Mox's belongings. "Where's the rest of your stuff, Mox?"

He rolled back over to the dresser and picked up his iPod Touch . "Right here."

"That's it?"

"This is all I need. Who is she?"

"That's Jennifer."

Jennifer waved.

"I don't know her."

"She's my friend, Mox... she's helpin' me get Brandi back."

The minute he heard Brandi's name, it was like everything was on pause and life went silent. He looked up at Priscilla, blinked and a single teardrop rolled down the side of his face. "I fucked up Priscilla..."

Mox, not now, we gotta get you outta here." A river of tears was building in her eye wells, but she managed to hold them back. "Jennifer, help me get him out that chair."

"I can't walk Priscilla..." he dropped his head in shame.

"Well, you're gonna start today." She draped one of his arms around her neck and Jennifer did the same. "Now stand up Mox."

He didn't even try. "I can't."

"Mox, don't tell me you can't. Stand up."

He conjured all the strength he could, and tried to stand on his own two feet, but it wasn't enough.

"I can't fuckin' do it, Priscilla!" Spit flew from his mouth and he let his body fall back into the wheelchair.

Priscilla snatched him by the collar of his t-shirt and got right in his face. "Don't fuckin' embarrass me in front of my friend." tears fell into Mox's lap. "Now stand up before I push you out this chair and leave you right here on this goddamn floor."

Mox was startled; he heard Priscilla use that tone before, but never with him.

His breathing got heavy, he tightened his jaw and he lifted himself out the chair just enough for Priscilla and Jennifer to hold him up.

"I told you. I knew you could do it, Mox."

Priscilla was happy that he hadn't given up, but she was also conscious of the effort, sacrifice and devotion it would take to reconstruct him.

They managed to get Mox onto the elevator, downstairs, through the lobby and into Jennifer's car.

The forty minute drive home was a silent one. Priscilla, with her seat back, gazed lazily out the window at passing traffic and Mox, leaned over in the backseat, slept most the way back, due to being under the influence of some pain medication he was prescribed.

When they arrived back at Jennifer's house, she helped Priscilla get Mox inside and then she got back into her car.

"You sure you don't need anything? I probably won't come back 'til the mornin'... I got some runnin' around to do."

"We're good." Priscilla replied. "Go 'head, take care of your business, we'll be fine."

"Alright... lata. Bye Mox."

Mox was propped up on the brown, leather sofa with agony etched on his face and chagrin in his heart.

Priscilla locked the door and then sat right next to him. "Mox," she put her hand underneath his chin and raised his head. "We gon' get through this baby. I want you to know that I'm here for you every step of the way, but you gotta help me out. You gotta focus every bit of energy you got into this recovery, and let go of the anger and resentment... that's the only way it's gonna happen."

Mox was aware of the exertion he needed to put forth in order to restore his mind and body; he was just praying that the devil hadn't captured his lost soul.

He reached over, grabbed Priscilla's hand and looked in her eyes. "Only God can bring me through this... it's his call."

The doorbell rang and it broke their concentration.

"Who is it?" Priscilla walked to the door, peeked through the peep hole and then unlocked it when she saw who it was.

"Good afternoon." A short, Spanish guy in a brown suit was holding a box. "I have a package for a Ms. Priscilla Davis."

She checked him out from head to toe. It looked like a UPS suit, but she knew it wasn't. "That's me." she said, reaching for the box.

"Here you go, m'am... have a nice day." He strolled off and got into a big brown truck.

Priscilla ripped a card off the top of the box and read it:

We're even now... let Mox know I said, get strong.

Enjoy...

Juan Carlos.

She carried the box to the living room and placed it on the coffee table in front of Mox.

"Who was that?" he questioned.

Priscilla tossed the card into his lap.

"*Even?* What is he talkin' about? What did you do Priscilla?"

She cracked the box open and dumped the contents on the table.

It was ten, individually wrapped kilograms of fishscale cocaine.

Priscilla smiled and nodded her head. "We back in business baby..."

CHAPTER FIFTEEN

A chill November breeze snuck through the cracked window of Tyrell's brand new black on black, Camaro SS. He looked around to see where it was coming from, and noticed the passenger side window was slightly open.

He tapped Six's chest with the back of his hand. "Yo, Six... Six... wake up nigga."

"Huh?..." Six wiped some slob from his bottom lip.

"Close my fuckin' window, you lettin' my heat out."

A tap on the driver's side window made Tyrell jump and he immediately reached for the gun under his seat.

The person on the outside of the car was saying something, but couldn't be heard because the window was still up.

He pressed the button and let it roll down.

"Goddamn it, old man... you 'bout to get ya' stupid ass shot."

The scraggly old timer had an ashy, ripped up, leather jacket on, old Levi jeans that looked like he'd been painting in them, and a pair of Timberland boots that were two sizes too big. His beard was haggard like he hadn't seen a barbershop in years, and what few teeth he had left in his mouth were rotted and discolored.

"You know I come bearin' information lil' nigga." He said.

Tyrell tossed the mean ice grill at the old jack. "What the fuck I tell you 'bout that lil' nigga shit, Trash Can…" he pulled the gun up and placed it on his lap.

"Call me by my name and I'll call you by yours."

"Mann… we call you Trash Can… 'cause you look like you jus' hopped out a muthafuckin' trash can, nigga!" Tyrell and Six keeled over with obnoxious laughter.

"Whenever you ready to cut the muthafuckin' jokes, I got some real shit to spit at cha…" Trash Can went to turn and walk off.

"Aye! Bring yo' ass over hea' nigga." Tyrell couldn't stop laughing. "Nah, for real… c'mere, wassup?" he was nearly wiping tears from his eyes.

Trash Can snatched the half of cigarette that was nestled in the bridge of his ear and lit it. “Fuck the word on the street… I seen it wit’ my own eyes.” He took a long drag and let the smoke funnel through his nostrils. “Your boy Leo back on the streets.”

They sat up in their seats at the same time.

“Fuck you talkin’ about?” Tyrell’s smile went flat and everything became serious.

“I aint talkin’ ‘bout shit. I jus’ told you, I saw the lil’ nigga.”

Tyrell opened the door and stepped out the car. “When?” he asked.

“Five minutes ago, in the Chinese restaurant; over there on Lincoln n’ North.”

“Lincoln n’ North… yo, Six… get in the driver’s seat.” Tyrell ran over to the passenger side, cocked his weapon and threw his hoodie on. “Aye, Trash Can!” he grabbed a knot of one hundred dollar bills out of his pocket and peeled one off. “Here.” he handed the bill to the old man. “Go get yo’ ass in the shower or somethin’ ya heard. You fuckin’ stink.”

Trash Can snatched the money out of Tyrell’s hand. “Fuck you, lil’ nigga. Go handle your business.”

Six and Tyrell rode around the block, parked in front of the laundromat across the street, and walked into the Chinese restaurant.

Leo was sitting at a table so immersed in his plate of food, that he hadn't even acknowledged that Tyrell and Six were there.

"Whaddup, nigga?"

The sound of Tyrell's voice startled Leo and he almost choked on a spoonful of rice. "Oh shit, wassup Tyrell?" he stood to give him a pound, but was ignored.

Tyrell squeezed into the seat right next to Leo and Six just stood there with a mean mug stuck on his face.

"You... when you get out?" he questioned, sensing the fear in Leo's movements.

"Umm... this mornin'. I was gon' come see you in a second, but I was starving,' I had to get something to eat."

Tyrell picked up a piece of Leo's chicken from out of his tray and bit it. "Is that right? Lemme ask you a question... and before you answer." He pulled the skin off with his teeth and tossed the bone back into the tray. "Please don't lie to me. How did you make bail?"

"Oh," Leo's nerves were jumping through his skin. He was listening to every word Tyrell was saying, but his attention was on Six and his ice grill. "Umm... my grandmother put up her crib for me."

Tyrell looked at Six and then back to Leo. "Your grandmother? Leo, you fuckin' lyin' I known you all my life and I know your whole family. Your grandmother died five years ago."

Leo tensed up. "I aint lyin' Rell, not my mother's mom, my father's mother, she lives in North Carolinia."

"I don't believe you Leo." Tyrell stood up. "I hope you ain't go out like a sucka."

"Huh? Man, Tyrell... I ain't got no reason to lie to you." Leo felt the tension.

Six butted in. "Everybody else doin' it."

"I ain't everybody else..." he responded. "Look Tyrell, we been friends since kindergarten... I know you don't think I told on you?"

"Did you?"

"Hell no!" Leo started breathing harder. "I would never do no shit like that."

Tyrell smirked. "Come take a ride wit' me Leo."

"C'mon, Rell... It aint even gotta be like this." Leo knew what 'Take a ride' meant.

"Leo," Tyrell shook his head. "Either you come willingly or by force... it don't matter to me."

Leo's expression was cheerless, he sensed the danger lurking. "Where we goin?'"

"Don't worry about it... I wanna show you somethin'." The three men walked out to the car. "Get in the front Leo." Six jumped in the backseat, Tyrell hit play on the radio and 2Pac's *Last Muthafucka Breathin* came through the speakers.

They rode on the highway for twenty minutes until Tyrell got off the exit and pulled over at an abandoned building on East 147th street in the Bronx.

Leo swallowed the lump in his throat and surveyed the area as they pulled into a vacant lot that housed a ramshackle building.

The volume on the radio went low and the only thing you could hear is the sound of the gravel under the slow rolling tires.

Tyrell came to a complete stop and looked over at Leo, he was scared to death sitting in the passenger seat. "Get out."

Leo took a deep breath and his right hand started twitching. "C'mon, Tyrell... please man..."

Six slapped him on the back of his head. "Shut yo' punk ass up and get the fuck out the car."

The three of them walked one hundred yards to the entrance of the abandoned building. It was torn down, ragged, and in need of some serious renovations.

"This shit crazy right." Tyrell tapped Leo's arm. "C'mon, let's go inside."

The inside of the building was worse off than the outside; cracked and shattered walls, a battered staircase, and a stench that could make your stomach turn and your eyes water.

Tyrell fished a rolled blunt from his pocket and put fire to it. "Member when we was kids, Leo... and you use to be rappin' all the time n' shit." he blew smoke into the air. "You still be rappin'?"

"Yeah." He answered.

"That's good. Check this out. In a few months, I'ma be investin' some money into this place. I'm thinkin' 'bout buildin' a studio and startin' a label."

Leo smiled. "For real?"

"Word, and I want you to be my first artist."

"Whew..." Leo sighed and looked up to God to thank him. "I thought you was bringin' me out here for somethin' else."

"Somethin' else?" Tyrell chuckled. "This nigga's buggin' Six. What... you thought I was bringin' you down here to kill or something nigga'?

Leo tried to laugh it off, but his heart was beating so fast he was about to have an attack and kill his self.

"Nah," he lied. "I'm jus' sayin'... we all the way down here; I didn't know what the fuck was goin' on." He laughed, but when he realized he was the only one, he stopped.

Tyrell shook his head. "You a scary ass nigga, Leo. Man, I would never do no shit like that to you, here." he passed him the blunt. "You my nigga right?"

Leo nodded his head up and down as he inhaled the potent weed smoke.

"Cool... yo," Tyrell started tapping his foot. "I gotta take a piss... I'll be right back." he trotted over to a dark corner.

"You rap too?"

Leo turned around and the barrel of a gun was pointed at his head.

Tyrell yelled from a distance. "Six hurry up!"

Leo was frozen stiff, his eyes halfway out the sockets. "Please don—"

The blast blew a piece of Leo's face off and he fell to the gravel.

Tyrell jogged back over. "Fuck is you waitin' for, shoot that nigga again."

Six complied.

"Took you long enough, nigga." Tyrell grabbed the gun from Six. "Gimmie my shit.

They got back into the car and drove away.

"Look," Jennifer pointed to a white and grey house at the corner of Cliff Avenue and 2nd Street. That's the house right there." she said as they cruised by.

"Go around again. I didn't see it." Priscilla lied.

"Girl, we can't be ridin' around in Pelham like this. These cops don't play."

"Alright, jus' one more time… please."

Jennifer circled the block a second time and Priscilla couldn't believe her eyes.

The front door of the house came open and Brandi stepped out followed by a middle aged white woman. *"Button your jacket Brandi, it's cold out."*

Priscilla heard the woman's voice and stared at Brandi's angelic face.

Jennifer was going 18 miles per hour, but it seemed like she was doing 5.

Priscilla wanted so bad to jump out of the car and wrap her precious child in her arms, but she couldn't; because she would delete any chances she had of getting her back.

"Look at my baby…" is all she could say as they floated by. She sniffled and did her best to hold herself from crying. "We gotta do something Jennifer. I can't go another day without my baby."

"What are we gonna do? It's too cold for them to be in the park." Jennifer replied.

Priscilla's mind was working in overdrive. "I got a plan..." she said. "I'm gonna get my baby back, whether they like it or not... she's mine."

2 HOURS LATER

"Where the hell you get these from?" Jennifer questioned, looking at herself in the mirror.

Priscilla was standing right next to her. "A friend lemme borrow them, crazy right?"

"Crazy ain't the word... these look jus' like UPS uniforms."

When Priscilla realized snatching Brandi from a public park would be too risky, she thought about the day Juan Carlos sent her the package and the disguise one of his men used. Once she got in contact with him, he wasted no time sending over two uniforms and a decoy truck to set the plan in motion.

"Hol' up... lemme practice." She pretended to knock on a door. "*Knock! Knock!*.. that's me knocking on the door right? Okay, so when they answer, I'ma be like... how you doin' m'am. I have a delivery for you today." Jennifer broke down laughing at herself.

"Wait. Wait..." Priscilla was laughing along with her. "If you do that, we definitely goin' to jail. But for real, c'mon let's get this over with because I been separated from my baby for too long."

Jennifer slowed up and pulled the big brown truck to the curb at 207 Cliff Avenue. "You sure this gon' work?" the nervousness was settling in.

"Jus' do exactly what I told you and everything is gonna be fine."

The two women exited the car and Jennifer went to the front door as planned while Priscilla tip toed around to the back of the house undetected.

After three knocks, she could hear someone coming to answer the door. "Who is it?" the woman asked.

"Umm... Umm... Delivery m'am! UPS!" she shouted.

The door started to come open.

Priscilla pulled a lock-pick out of her pocket, slid it into the key hole and jiggled it until the door popped open.

She moved cautiously through the dark kitchen, past the dining room and into the living quarters, very careful of knocking something over. The television was on, but nobody was downstairs to watch it. Priscilla heard Jennifer holding a conversation with the middle aged white woman.

"So, you sure you didn't order this, because this is your address right." Jennifer backed up and glimpsed at the number on the front of the house. "Yup, 207."

The woman said, "Yes, that's my address, but I didn't order that."

Jennifer was stalling the best she could, wishing Priscilla would hurry up. "Well, m'am... I don't know what to tell ya'. If I was you, I would jus' take it. Hey, they're the ones who sent it to the wrong address."

Priscilla eased up the staircase and went to check the first room to the right of her. She gently turned the knob and pushed the door open just enough to see if anyone was in it. When she saw it was empty, she moved to the next few rooms that were about ten feet down the hallway.

The next two produced nothing, but it looked like somebody was in the bed of the fourth room, so Priscilla sneakily entered.

She tugged on the cover and the occupant of the bed rolled over.

It was Brandi.

Priscilla snatched the cover off when she saw it was her and tapped her leg. "Brandi... Brandi, wake up, it's mommy."

Brandi adjusted her eyes to the faint light, looked into her mother eyes and smiled. "Mommy, I miss you."

Priscilla picked her up from the bed and gave her the warmest, fondest hug she could give. She breathed deep and thanked God for putting her child back into her arms.

"Mommy missed you too, baby…" Her tears fell like drops of rain in a severe thunderstorm.

Brandi's excitement suddenly turned to a look of fear. "I don't like it here mommy…"

"Okay, baby… mommy's takin' you home."

Holding Brandi in her clutches as if her life depended on it, Priscilla quietly dipped back through the hallway and headed for the stairs.

A toilet flushed and the creaking of a door opening caused Priscilla to stop in her tracks.

"Rose, is that you!?" A male voice shouted.

Priscilla heard footsteps and took off down the staircase, darted through the living room and escaped out the back door.

Jennifer kept peeking past the woman's shoulder trying to see if everything was alright and she caught a glimpse of Priscilla rushing through the back of the house. She wrapped her conversation up instantly. "Well, if you don't want it, fuck it… I'll take it. Have a great night. Bye!"

CHAPTER SIXTEEN

Christmas of 2011 came quicker than virgin in his first piece of pussy. It was the same day, one year ago that Mox was reunited with Priscilla and discovered he had a daughter named Brandi, only to have Priscilla disappear like a crack head in debt to a dope boy.

Since then, everything had taken a turn for the worse and Mox was on the bad end of a long stick, but the complications he endured within the last 365 days had brought him to where he was today; still breathing, a man with dignity, morals and a heart of stone. Determined, dedicated and disciplined, Mox was again ready to take to the streets, only this time, he didn't plan on losing.

Once Priscilla rescued him from the rehab center, Mox's recovery became much smoother. Of course, there were times when he really wanted to quit, but then that sweet, heavenly smile that Brandi wore pushed all thoughts of giving up out the window.

Reconditioning himself was far from an easy task and without the help of Priscilla and Jennifer; Mox may not have made it.

The days when his body completely shut down and he couldn't move, Priscilla was there; bathing him, feeding him and making sure he took his prescribed medicines.

At times, it got so bad that Mox would unconsciously go to the bathroom on himself and Priscilla wouldn't question cleaning him up. She was there step for step with him while he strengthened his body and began to walk and exercise. She read books to him every night; books like, *The 48 Laws of Power, The Art of War, The Prince* and many more. Not only did she assist in his physical reconstruction, but also his mental reformation.

She was building Mox up; building him up to be the man that God had destined him to be; a leader; a doer and not just another nigga with power. A wise man, a strong man; a family man...

With the return of Brandi, Mox and Priscilla's bond grew daily because they were able to interact with each other frequently. It was the first time in Brandi's life that both her mother and father were in the same household and it was beginning to feel like a real family.

Mox turned the water off and stepped out the shower. He eyed himself in the foggy mirror and smiled. His weight was up and his daily workouts were showing major results.

He snatched a towel off the rack, wrapped it around his lower body and went to leave out the bathroom when a knock on the door startled him; and then it came open.

"Oh shoot! Excuse me..." Jennifer burst in the door. Her eyes were stuck on Mox's glistening chiseled pecks. "Umm, nice chest." She grinned and slammed the door shut.

Even though Jennifer was kind enough to let the trio crash at her house, Mox wasn't too keen on making a new friend in her. It was something about Jennifer that he just couldn't put his finger on, but in due time, he would find out.

Mox walked out the bathroom and into the room that he and Priscilla were occupying.

"I don't like your friend Jennifer." He said.

Priscilla got up from the bed and put her arms around his neck. "Mox, you don't like anybody. She kissed him on his cheek. "How could you not like her, she's helped us out so much."

"At what cost, Priscilla?"

"Mox don't be like that. Brandi enjoys her company."

"Keep that bitch away from my daughter. You hear me?" When she didn't respond, he said it louder. "You hear me!?"

"Yes, Mox... damn, bite my head off."

"I'm not playin' Priscilla. I don't want her around my daughter."

"That's gonna be kinda hard being that were stayin' in *her* house, Mox."

A bang at the door startled them and Jennifer walked in the room like she had seen a ghost. "Oh my fuckin' God! Look at this shit." she picked the remote up, hit power and turned to the local news.

They almost missed it.

Once again, Priscilla Davis is wanted for questioning regarding the kidnapping of her seven year old daughter, Brandi Davis, who was in the custody of her foster parents at the time of the abduction. Any information or tips on the whereabouts of Ms. Davis, please call 555-CRIME-STOPPERS.

Mox just shook his head. "*Kidnapping?* We gotta get outta here."

"Where are we gonna go Mox?" Priscilla was still in awe of seeing her mug shot plastered on the television screen.

"I don't know, but we gotta make a move. Where's Brandi?"

Jennifer replied. "She's downstairs. Hey guys, my friend has this place upstate. It's vacant, it's paid for and there ain't no neighbors in site for two miles. Y'all can crash there if you want to."

Priscilla looked at Mox. "What you think?"

He side eyed her.

"Where is it Jennifer?"

"About three hours north, in the Catskills."

Mox turned his lip up. "In the mountains? Oh hell no... I aint goin' back up in them mountains. You must be crazy."

"Mox," Prsicilla tried to convince him. "We don't have many options."

"There's always another option." He said. "I want y'all to stay in the house. I gotta go see somebody. Priscilla, let me get your keys."

"Mox, you shouldn't be drivin'."

"I'm fine, trust me..."

She tossed her car keys to him and he walked out the door.

For the first time in four and a half months, Mox was about to step foot onto the same streets that almost ended his life. The same streets that he showed so much love to, but in the end, there was never any reciprocation; the same streets that claimed the lives of his most cherished loved ones, leaving him to feel vanquished and uncertain of his own future; these same streets he called home; that he'd been absent from for days on end, but now, he was ready; he was prepared, willing, determined and overly eager to make his reappearance a grandiose one, and that's exactly what he was going to do.

Priscilla didn't want him to go, but she knew he wouldn't listen. "Be careful Mox." was all she could tell him.

Mox got behind the wheel of Priscilla's 2011, black Audi A8 and adjusted his seating. It felt like forever since he had driven a car, but as soon as he hit the ignition, it was like he hadn't lost a day.

He admired the cars exquisite detailing and the plushness of the fine, autumn colored, bull hide, leather seats; it was like sitting in the cock pit of a G5 Jet.

As he navigated the streets in route to his destination, Mox repeatedly glanced up at the rearview mirror catching sight of the patch that covered his eye. He was trying to get used to it, but with each brief look his heart grew heavy and cold.

When he reached his destination, he valet parked the car and then walked into the apartment building on a surprise visit.

"Who is it, goddamn it!" Earl shouted when he heard someone knocking on the door.

"It's me, Unc... open up."

Earl caught wind of the voice and smiled big. "I know that ain't who I think it is..." he unlocked the door and could have sworn he was dreaming. "Nephew!" he grabbed Mox's shoulders and brought him in close to hug him. "Man... you don't know how much I missed yo' ass boy."

"I missed you too, Unc."

"Yeah, man... c'mon in here."

Mox looked around at the stylish, yet modern set up Wise Earl had. "This is nice, Unc. I'm proud of you."

"Thanks man... glad you like it. Sheeiit... goddamn rent two thousand dollars a month. If you ask me, they need to have a few more amenities in this muthafucka." he chuckled.

"I see you on your Don Juan Chino shit, huh?"

Earl smirked, rubbed his beard and then fixed the belt on his silk robe. "A lil' sumptin' sumptin'... Have a seat, I wanna introduce you to somebody." He swaggered off to the back room.

Mox took a seat on the leather sectional couch that was in the middle of the living room. He surveyed the wall hangings and one picture in particular caught his attention. He quickly hopped up and went over to give it a closer look.

Earl appeared from the back room. "Nephew, meet Baby G... my fiancé."

When he turned around, he was shocked.

Baby G wasn't a baby in any way, shape, form or fashion.

She was 5 feet 2 inches tall, dark chocolate skin, long black hair and cake that could feed a party of a hundred.

"Hi Mox." She said. Her voice was soft and prissy.

"Wassup." He couldn't help but to stare. "I see you got you a young one, huh Unc?"

Earl poured himself a shot of Cognac from his mini bar next to the dining room. He sniffed the yak and swirled it in his glass. "Yeah, she may be young, but goddamnit she ain't dumb... ain't that right baby."

Mox took his seat back on the couch. "So wassup Unc. What the streets lookin' like?"

"You know how these streets is, Mox." Earl sat in his leather recliner chair directly across from his nephew and lit a cigarette. "These young niggas fuckin' up the game, right now. They out here shootin' everything movin'."

"Word... it's like that huh? I got a plan though, Unc... the perfect plan."

"You know as well as I know, ain't no such thing as the perfect plan. You gotta get what yours and get the hell out. It's that simple."

Earl reached under the recliner and pulled out a Gucci messenger bag. He tossed it to Mox.

"What's this?"

"A lil' token of my appreciation for all the love you showed me through the years." He blew smoke into the air.

Mox unzipped the bag and pulled out a black jewelry box. He opened it.

"Ohhh... this is nice." He eyed the white gold and diamond pinky ring. "This for me Unc?"

"Yeah. There's something else in there too."

He put his hand back into the bag and came out with a stack of one hundred dollar bills. "This what I'm talkin' 'bout." he said, holding the stack of bills in front of him. "This shit right here rules the world. They say it ain't everything, but I've come to learn that you can't do nothin' without it."

"You right about that, nephew. So what you gon' do? I see they got Priscilla's face all over the news. How's the baby girl?"

"I gotta get a spot so she can lay low. I need to make some moves Unc. I don't trust these niggas no more... I need your help."

"You gon' find Priest?"

Mox stuffed the cash back into the bag. "You know I am... but first, I wanna find that nigga Cleo."

CHAPTER SEVENTEEN

SUMTER, SOUTH CAROLINA

"It's dark as fuck out here, Chris." Cleo looked to the passenger seat and Chris' head was tilted against the window. He was snoring like a bear. "Yo, Chris." he tapped his leg. "Chris wake up, we here."

Cleo made the right into the driveway of 1648 Radical Road and put the car in park.

The house was a single story flat, built on three acres of land and it was right next to the woods.

He sat in the pitch blackness debating whether he should go in or not. The pit of his stomach was rumbling and his palms were building up with sweat by the seconds.

What if she didn't even live here anymore? he thought.

"You goin' in?"

He jumped when he heard Chris' voice. "Don't scare me like that." Cleo turned the car off. "Yeah, wait here while I go see wassup. And get in the driver's seat. It's your turn."

Cleo got out the car, fixed the gun on his waist and walked down the driveway to the front of the house. He could barely see in front of him, and he nearly tripped climbing the four steps leading to the front door.

The sounds at night time in the country were much different than sounds after dark in the city. Cleo wasn't excited about being in town for too long.

He knocked on the door loud enough for someone to hear it, but there was no answer, so he knocked a second time, and again, there was no answer. He went to leave and a latch opened on the door.

It was a woman's voice. "Who you come here to see?"

Cleo spun on his heels and looked at the woman wearing a night gown, standing in her doorway.

She looked exactly like the pictures, beautiful.

For a second, Cleo got lost in her loveliness. He couldn't believe how much he resembled her. A thought ran across his mind and he wanted to become a kid again, so he could leap into her arms, give her a great big hug and tell her that he loved her, but in actuality; his heart held a massive amount of hate towards her.

"It's me, ma... your son." Cleo said.

The woman pushed the screen door open and stepped onto the porch to get a better look at this man claiming to be her son.

"I ain't got no son. You at the wrong house, now get off my porch." she replied.

Cleo knew she was lying. She looked exactly like the woman in the picture he had in his hand. "So, your name aint Vivian?"

"No, my name ain't Vivian... now I ain't gon' tell you again."

Cleo held up the picture. "This ain't you?"

She squinted her eyes to get a better look at the picture and the way she reacted told the truth. "Where'd you get that from?" she questioned.

"Sybil gave it me."

Silence settled in.

"I'm sorry Cleo..." she finally admitted.

He screwed his face up. "Yeah, you are sorry, a sorry excuse for woman."

"Cleo don—"

"Don't Cleo me... How the hell you know my name anyway?"

Vivian fixed her gown and sat in the wicker chair that was on the porch. "Sybil and I kept in contact until you were three years old. She would send me pictures every Christmas. Listen, Cleo... I know you're upset and you have every right to be, but we're here now and we can start over."

"Start over?" Cleo laughed. "Lady, you musta bumped yo' goddamn head. You abandoned me... left me wit' one of your friends and never came back to check on me... not even once." his eyes started to get glossy and his lip quivered. "You wanna start over? We never started anything to begin with." The tears slid down his face. "The day I found that letter was the worst day of my life, and from that day on, I capsuled so much anger, that after a while, I just exploded." He mimicked an explosion with his hands. "People say I'm losin' my mind..." Cleo's grin turned sinister. "More and more I'm startin' to agree wit' them..."

"Well, if you don't want to start over, why are you here?" she asked.

"I'm here for closure..." Cleo turned his back on her and walked away.

"Cleo, come back..." She called out, but he kept walking.

When he got back in the car he laid his head back on the headrest and let his eyes close.

"You alright?" Chris started the car.

Cleo opened his eyes, sat up and looked at Chris. "Nah… hol' up." he pushed the door open, walked back to the house and knocked on the door.

"Cleo, is that you?"

He answered. "Yeah."

When the door opened, Cleo lifted his gun and pointed it at her face.

She opened her mouth, but nothing came out.

He gripped the weapon tight keeping a steady aim. "You the reason I'm not able to love. You fucked my life up."

He closed his eyes and squeezed the trigger.

Three shots.

CHAPTER EIGHTEEN

Mox sat patiently on the couch and waited for Frank to give him a reasonable answer.

"I'm waitin' Frank."

"Mox, I told you, I was busy."

"Busy? You was too busy to come see me in the hospital, that's what you tellin' me?"

"I got a business to run."

"Fuck your business Frank!" Mox was furious. "I was dyin' in that muthafucka and you niggas was sittin' back countin' money!"

Nate tried to reason. "It wasn't like that Mox."

"Well what was it then, tell me... because from what I see ain't too much work been getting done. Where the fuck is Cleo?"

"Mox, we been looking for him..." Frank explained. "Even put the young kid, Tyrell on him... nothing."

Mox paced the rug in Frank's living room. "I expected more from y'all. We supposed to be a union, a team. What happened to that?"

"Nothing happened Mox. We still are a union." Frank replied.

Mox picked his leather jacket up, put it on, and opened the door. "Are we?"

The feelings Mox had toward his brothers were bittersweet. He was unsettled and disturbed at the fact the he'd been hospitalized for months and they hadn't taken the time to see if he was okay. He felt like when things took a turn for the worse, the only people by his side were Priscilla and Uncle Earl, and those were the people he least expected.

There was still plenty of unfinished business to be handled, but Mox was no longer relying on anyone other than himself to take care of it. He would handle things on his own from here on out.

He jumped in the Audi, hit the ignition and stepped on the gas.

Light snow flurries descended from sky and the brisk February winds tugged at Tyrell and Six's face as they stood in front of the building.

"You fucked shorty last night?" Tyrell was being nosy.

"You know I did." Six laughed. "Her and her friend."

"Yeah right nigga, you lyin'."

"Scouts honor."

Tyrell didn't believe him. "Man, fuck a scouts honor… put that shit on yo' momma so I know it's real." He didn't realize what he said until seconds later. "Ohh shit… my bad. I ain't mean nothin' behind that."

"It is what it is Rell… she gone now, ain't shit I can do about it." Six passed Tyrell half of a cigarette.

"You a strong ass nigga, B. Even though me and my moms don't get along, I think I might fuckin' bugg out if I was to lose her."

"I feel you… Yo, who this nigga?"

A man in a black flight jacket approached them. "Excuse me, Tyrell?"

"Yeah, wassup?" Tyrell had his hand on his gun.

"I'm Leo's father, Mr. Smalls…"

He eased his hand off the weapon. "Oh yeah, Mr. Smalls, I remember you."

"I've been looking for you to ask you if you've seen Leo since he came home?"

"He's home?" Tyrell played the dummy role.

"Yeah, my mother put up her house for him to get out. He has court in the morning and no one has seen him."

Tyrell and Six looked at each other.

"Nah, I ain't seen him around here. If I do, I'll let him know you're lookin' for him."

"Thank you. I appreciate it." Mr. Smalls stepped off.

Six turned his head to Tyrell. "You fucked up..."

CHAPTER NINTEEN

Mox let the hot water run on his back while he pondered his next move. Uncle Wise found out that Priest had been released from prison and was back to his old ways, so it wouldn't be too hard to catch up to him. He also discovered that Cleo was hiding out in the south somewhere, trying to blend in with the country folk.

Mox envisioned the day he would finally get the chance to see his father eye to eye and he could feel his hands wrapping around his throat, choking the life out of him.

The memories hadn't gone anywhere and Mox's hate towards his father only grew stronger.

He pulled the shower curtain back when he heard the bathroom door open. "Who is that?"

Priscilla walked in, dropped her towel and stepped in the shower with him.

She wrapped her arms around Mox's neck and stuffed her tongue in his mouth.

Her saliva was warm, savory and sweet like honey.

He reached down and slid his middle finger into her saturated kitten and tickled her clitoris with his thumb.

"Ohh Mox, I'm 'bout to cum..."

She revolved her hips on his finger until her cream dripped down the side of his hand.

Mox pulled his finger out and licked the juices. "Umm you taste good..."

Priscilla reached down and brushed his manhood until it was solid and then guided him into her wetness.

The hot water beating on their bodies was soothing and sensual.

Mox pinned her back against the tile and submerged himself deep within in her love.

He stroked her kitty slow, long, and hard.

"Yes Mox... ohhh..."

She felt his body stiffen and his muscles jumped.

"I'm cumin baby..."

Priscilla compressed her vaginal walls and pulled the cum out of Mox.

"Oh sheeiiit!" He grabbed her by the waist tightly and let it all go inside of her.

When they finished, they washed each other and went to get in the bed.

Priscilla's head was on Mox's chest. "Do you love me Mox?"

He smiled. "Of course I do. Why would you ask that?"

"Because..." She was afraid to say it.

"Because what?"

Priscilla didn't want to start an argument, and if she said something, that's exactly what would happen. But this particular issue had been on her mind for a few days now and she wanted answers.

"Who's Jasmine?"

Mox was surprised to hear her name.

"That's the nurse that was lookin' after me when I was in the hospital."

"Why do you have her number?"

Why you goin' through my shit?"

Priscilla was getting upset. "Mox I asked you a question."

Mox knew the question she really wanted to ask, and if so, he was prepared to lie.

"So you not gonna answer me?"

"What you want me to tell you Priscilla?"

She sat up against the headboard. "I want you to tell me the truth Mox. Are you fuckin' her?"

Mox shook his head. "Nah." he lied. Since his return home, he had been to see Jasmine twice.

"You lying Mox."

"You asked me a question, I told you the answer and now I'm lying?" He pushed the covers off and got out the bed. "You know... it's hurts me to think that you don't believe me."

"Well, you know what hurts even more, Mox?... watching the person you love, fall in love with someone else and ain't nothing you can do about it. That shit hurts."

Priscilla's eyes started to water. "I spoke to her Mox, she told me everything."

"I don't know what you talkin' about."

"She told me how she took care of you and how y'all got together when you came home. All this shit about you wanting to be with her and you wanna get away from all this bullshit in your life... is that what I am to you Mox... bullshit?"

"Priscilla..."

"I've done everything for you Mox. I showed you how to play this game. I was there for you when you were locked up, when you got shot and through the recovery, and in return you give me your ass to kiss."

"Priscilla..."

"No, fuck you Mox." She pulled the covers over her head and went to sleep.

Priest checked his Bulova watch. “It’s almost that time boys. Y’all ready?” he reached into the bag he was carrying and pulled out four masks.

“What the hell are those Priest?”

“We going with something different this time fellas, no more movie stars... we mobsters today.”

Two weeks ago Priest had been released from state prison and he was already about to pull his third bank heist. He and his three cronies were stashed in a basement about a half a block away from the HSBC bank on Tarrytown Road in White Plains. If everything went as planned, Priest would come off with at least two million in cash.

“Here, take this, Slick.” He passed him the John Gotti mask.

Slick said, “Okay... I get to be Gotti for the day.”

“Here Mel.” Priest tossed Mel the Vinny the Chin mask.

“This is that Vinny the Chin muhfucka, right?”

Priest answered. “Yeah, that’s him.”

“Yo, Que... this you.” He handed Que the Sammy the Bull mask.

Que couldn’t figure out who it was. “Who the fuck is this?”

Mel took it out of his hand, looked at it and started laughing. "That's the rat... Sammy the Bull!" he laughed louder. "You gotta be the rat!"

"Nah, fuck that Priest... why I gotta wear the rat joint?"

Mel couldn't stop laughing.

"Coolout, Mel. Que, it don't matter what mask you get, just put the shit on."

Que was tight. "Man... I aint wearin' that, fuck that."

Priest got in Que's face. "Put the fuckin' mask on."

Que saw how serious he was, and complied. Plus Priest was probably a hundred pounds heavier, so a fight was out of the question anyway.

"Lemme see your gun, Que."

Que passed Priest his .9 millimeter.

"Now see... you look good as Sammy the rat!" Priest cocked the gun back and emptied the clip in his chest. "Anybody else feel like talkin' to the police... alright then... proceed."

CHAPTER TWENTY

Since their argument, Mox had been holding the couch down for the last few days in Jennifer's living room. She didn't mind; her home was their home until they figured out where they wanted to live.

During the day, Jennifer did a lot of running around so she was rarely ever at the house, but recently she claimed to be on vacation from work and decided to lounge out at the crib.

"Wassup Mox?" she tried to strike up a conversation.

Mox sat back on the couch, flicking through cable channels. "I'm chillin', wassup wit' you?"

"Nothing much." Jennifer sat down next to him on the couch. "Can I see your eye?"

Mox ignored her.

"Look, I know you don't like me, but I think if you get to know me, you'll think different." She tried to rub his leg, but he pushed her hand away.

"You buggin'."

"Am I? I know you and Priscilla goin' through y'all shit. I'm sayin' we can keep this between us."

"Keep what between us?"

"Whatever we do. If you don't tell, I won't tell." she responded.

"You ain't shit. I knew you was a snake the day I met you."

Jennifer stuck out her tongue and wiggled it like a snake would do.

"I know you wanna fuck me, Mox. I see the way you undress me wit' your eyes."

She stood up, pulled her sweatshirt off, and straddled Mox.

"Jennifer, get off me before Brandi wakes up and comes down here." He tried to push her off, but she wouldn't budge.

Mox's cell phone rang.

He looked at it, lying on the coffee table. It was Uncle Earl.

The front door opened, it was Priscilla.

The first things she saw were Jennifer's C-cups bouncing and the back of Mox's head.

"What the fuck!" She dropped the bag of groceries in her hand.

Mox turned his head, saw it was Priscilla, and pushed Jennifer off his lap.

His cell phone kept ringing.

Jennifer didn't bother covering up. "Wassup Priscilla?"

Mox picked his phone up. "Hello?"

Uncle Earl was on the other end. "The white bitch is poison! She a Telesco!"

"What!?" he dropped the phone and looked at Jennifer.

Priscilla's tears were falling like Alicia Key's hit single. She snatched the gun from the small of her back. "I'm not gon' let you hurt me no more." she aimed it at Mox.

Mox grabbed the pistol from his waistline and pointed it at Jennifer. "This bitch is settin' us up Priscilla!"

Priscilla's hands were trembling as she steadied the barrel to Mox head. "No more lies Mox."

"Priscilla put the gun down! Do you even know who this bitch is?"

Mox knew he recognized Jennifer from somewhere, she was Mikey T's little sister. He recalled seeing her in a home portrait years back when they played ball together.

"I don't care Mox... it doesn't matter anymore. Nothing matters. I did all I can do." She moved in closer.

Mox had his gun at Jennifer's head and Priscilla had her gun to Mox's head.

Jennifer joked. "Look at this, the perfect love triangle."

"Shut the fuck up!" Mox screamed. "Where your ID at?" he picked her bag up and dumped it on the carpet.

Her ID card landed by Priscilla's foot.

"Pick it up, Priscilla… tell me what it says."

Jennifer was trying to figure out a way to make a move. "He's lying Priscilla. He's jus' tryin to cover up the fact that we've been fuckin' since he came here."

"Don't believe her Priscilla. What does the card say!?" Mox's grip on the gun was getting tighter.

Prisiclla picked up the ID card. She read it slowly. "Jenn-i-fer Tel-es-co…"

She dropped the card.

"Daddy!!"

"Mox!"

A shot went off…

THE UNION 3 COMING SOON!

Made in the USA
San Bernardino, CA
06 March 2014